To Marie

SCIONS OF THE BLACK LOTUS

Virginia's blossoms are best.

THORN OF THE NIGHT BLOSSOMS

A Legends of Tivara Story

JC KANG RVA

To Fans of Jie. You Made This Happen

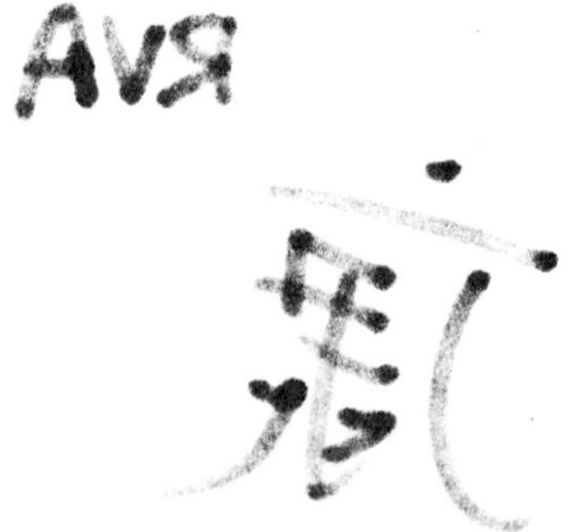

http://jckang.dragonstonepress.us

jc.kang.author@gmail.com

Cover Art by Binh Hai

Maps by Laura Kang

Logos by Emily Jose Burlingame

CONTENTS

MAPS

TIVARALAN

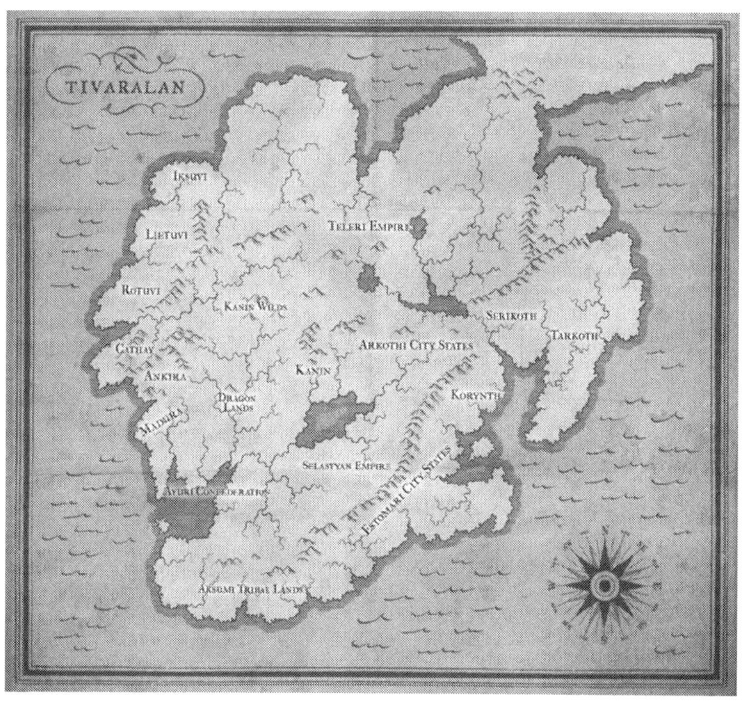

CATHAY

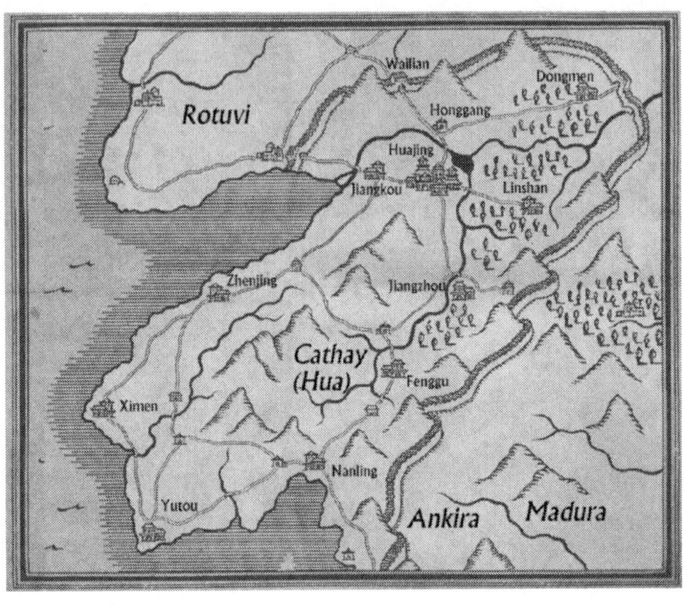
Waiian
Dongmen
Rotuvi
Honggang
Huajing
Jiangkou
Linshan
Zhenjing
Jiangzhou
Cathay
(Hua)
Fenggu
Ximen
Nanling
Yutou
Ankira
Madura

THE CAPITAL

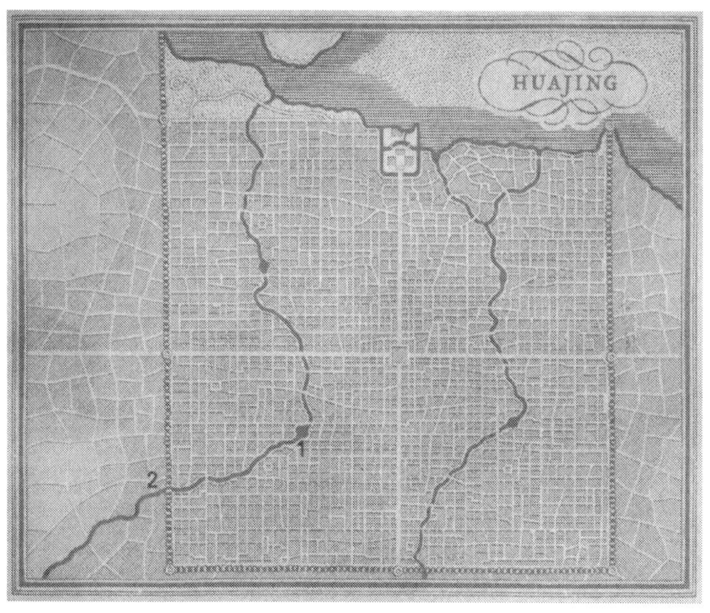

1. THE FLOATING WORLD
2. THE TRENCH

CHAPTER 1

The ongoing bid on Jie's virginity had already exceeded the highest recorded, in part because every other Night Blossom was claimed by sixteen. While seedy whorehouses in dingy back alleys dealt in whatever flesh a man with coin craved, and didn't necessarily keep accurate records, the Floating World's unwritten conventions stipulated that a Blossom remain unplucked before she flowered with Heaven's Dew. At twenty, Jie had extra years to catch the eye of wealthy men with her exotic features, and to her lament, had yet to bleed.

Unless she counted the cuts and scratches from her *other* training. She didn't, because even the stodgiest accountant in the Floating World would've needed an abacus to tally them all up.

Said grey-haired accountant happened to work as Florist for Jie's House, the Chrysanthemum Pavilion.

Ju Wei now looked from the shopping list to her ledger on her office's rosewood desk, illuminated by the morning sun through an oval window. She gave an appreciative nod. "You bought ten bottles of rice wine for a silver *jiao*?"

Actually, Jie had haggled with the brewery for a dozen and gotten two copper *fen* in change. All it took was the right pout, and the man was paper ready to be folded by dexterous fingers. "Yes, Florist." She bowed, the motion still too awkward by a Night Blossom's standards.

Florist Wei laughed, bright and clear for her middling age. "The House might make more sending you shopping than attracting Hummingbirds. Now, run along. I mean, off you go. *No* running."

Jie bowed again. She turned and reached for the sliding door.

"Ahem." Wei's tone carried loving exasperation.

With a bow no better than the last, Jie knelt at the door and slid it open. Once she'd stood, passed through, and bowed, she knelt again and closed the door. It was such a tedious ritual, one which the full-fledged Blossoms didn't have to perform at this hour, after the guests had left the House. As a Floret, Jie was bound by the tedium.

She glided over the nightingale floors, not making a sound. In all the Floating World's reputable Houses, the chirping floorboards allowed the Gardener to hear every coming and going, and help protect the Hummingbirds' anonymity. In a lord's castle, they were meant to deter spies.

Jie suppressed a laugh. All spies from the Black Lotus Clan learned to navigate the joists and joints as soon as they could walk. It required grace, though a different kind than that of the Night Blossoms of the Floating World. The only reason the lords of the realm thought nightingale floors worked was that no adept had ever been caught.

With her chores done, she headed to the only Blossom of the Chrysanthemum Pavilion not getting her beauty rest. As she moved down the hall, she kept her eyes set forward to avoid looking directly at the hanging scrolls of calligraphy and brush paintings. Created by Dragonscribes, their magic would cause an unsuspecting viewer to loosen their purse strings. Then again, most of the unsuspecting were usually too busy ogling the Blossoms to notice the art.

A full-fledged Night Blossom worked a very different kind of magic to achieve similar results, and few did better than the Chrysanthemum Pavilion's Corsage, Ju Lilian. How coincidental that the House nicknamed her *Beautiful Lotus*, never knowing her alter ego as the most beautiful Fist of the secret Black Lotus Clan.

Jie padded up the steps and crept down the hall to Lilian's room. Ear to the door, she listened, just to confirm that Beautiful Lotus' important patron had indeed left.

With Lilian's mastery of the *Viper's Skin*, her shallow breaths would've been inaudible even to most clan adepts. But not to Jie, with the tapered ears inherited from her worthless elf father; the same father whose blood slowed her aging and sped up her healing. It kept all but major lacerations from scarring, but also prevented Heaven's Dew from arriving.

Of course, Lilian didn't have to know whether anyone heard her or not. She lay in wait, suspended from the rafters on the other side of the door. As much fun as it would be to wait until her arms and legs got tired, an exhausted Fist endangered clan operations. Forgoing ceremony, Jie slid the door open and feigned unawareness as she stepped in....

...and spun out of the way, arcing a kick into the edge of the door in the same motion. Just enough force that it slid to a quiet shut.

Lilian landed right behind where Jie would've been, back exposed, without a sound on the plush wool carpet.

With equal silence, Jie swept a leg behind Lilian while wrapping an arm around her neck. She twisted her hips and sent the Blossom into a soundless heap on the ground. Rolling over, throwing her legs across Lilian's chest, she arched her back and locked Lilian in an armbar. Their silk gowns tangled in a flash of blues, yellows, and greens.

"Big Sister," Jie said in a loud voice. Although the thick walls and dense doors muted all but the loudest gasps and moans, Night Blossoms had a propensity for hearing things. Even with their reputation for discretion, the less they knew about the Black Fists in their midst, the better.

"Greetings, Little Floret." Lilian kept her voice even through gritted teeth. Any more leverage would dislocate her elbow.

Jie leaned back to apply a little more pressure. "I'm here for my lesson." If only it were true.

"You're late." Face red, Lilian surrendered with staccato taps on Jie's leg.

"My apologies, Big Sister." With a grin, Jie relented. She rolled backward into a crouch, fist to the ground, and stood.

"I appreciate your sincerity." Lilian's skirts billowed out as she twirled her legs like a windmill, vaulting herself upward feet-first and then landing. It was utterly immodest. Using clan hand signals, she signed, *You're not sorry at all, Big Sister.*

Not at all, Jie signaled back. She stood and placed her right fist in her left hand in a warrior's salute. "Please, teach me."

Lilian returned the gesture, adding a bow of her head. To the Chrysanthemum Pavilion, she was a full-fledged Blossom, the Corsage of the House; but she'd been an orphan of three when the Black Lotus Temple had adopted her, and six-year-old Jie had taken her under her wing.

She looked up from her bow.

What Lilian lacked in martial skill, she made up for in an elegance Jie hadn't deigned to master. Her thin, high-bridged nose accentuated large brown eyes. Glossy black hair, tousled first by entertaining an important guest the night before, and now by a more lethal form of grappling, framed her triangular face. At eighteen, she boasted ample curves.

A pit formed in Jie's throat. She'd been the Elder Sister, but still had a flat body, and was no closer to earning the clan her Plucking bid and leaving the Floating World. With a possible insurrection brewing in the North, the posturing and backstabbing of hereditary lords seemed much more interesting than the posturing and backstabbing of the entertainment district's great Houses.

Lilian motioned toward the bed. "Come. We'll practice the *Jade Polishing* technique."

Jie's belly fluttered. *Jade Polishing*—a euphemism for some sex act, but for what? A Blossom had a plethora of techniques at her disposal, all which *looked* titillating, but the silly names had never been her priority. After all, she'd eventually return to the Black Lotus Temple to train new recruits in stealth, fighting, and poisons; or maybe even get sent on missions to eliminate threats to the realm.

Then again, she'd already been in the House four years longer than originally planned, and her body ached for release in more ways than one.

Whereas they'd taken care to keep their martial interaction silent, both relaxed as they walked across the room. Lilian looked paler than usual, and dark bags hung under her eyes. Usually the embodiment of grace, it seemed as if she were slogging through mud.

Are you all right? Jie's fingers danced out the signs.

Lilian perked up, smiling and nodding.

All contrived. Her guest last night, perhaps? All the great Houses of the Floating World knew of Lord Ting's penchant for a little rough play. There were certainly worse Hummingbirds, and the most recalcitrant men had earned a ban from the Floating World altogether. No amount of money in the empire could buy reentry.

Jie looked around for clues. At a casual glance, nothing looked out of place in the room. The landscape paintings—one imbued with magic to loosen a viewer's lips—hung in their usual places on the wall. A red lacquer platter with a porcelain decanter and matching eggshell cups sat on a low table to the side. From the scent, a sour plum had flavored the rice wine. Lilian's bedsheets were appropriately rumpled, and the rug had shifted a degree, but that came as no surprise given Lord Ting's vigor.

Gut twisting at the thought of having to share Lilian, Jie swallowed hard.

Lilian's honeysuckle fragrance clung the strongest in the center of the carpet and the west side of the bed, mingling with fresh incense and the dissipating odor of sour man-sweat. It didn't take much imagination to picture what Lord Ting had done, and where. Another scent lingered, hidden among the others: *yinghua* flowers, a contact toxin that made most males susceptible to questions, and left them with a forgetful hangover.

Did you find anything out from Lord Ting? Jie signed.

Nodding, Lilian knelt by the bed. She slid a hand between the futon and frame and withdrew a finger-length tube. "Lie down."

Excitement jolted up Jie's spine, and she settled back into the cool softness of thick blankets.

Full report here, Lilian signed as she plopped down beside her and passed the tube over. "Relax."

Something was wrong. Lilian's tone and posture lacked enthusiasm. Excitement melting away, Jie sat up. It didn't look like they'd be practicing *Jade Carving*, whatever it was. She took the tube and slid it into the hidden pocket sewn into her sleeve. *What's it say?*

Lords of the North are grumbling. "That's better. See?"

Jie let out a moan for anyone who might happen to be listening at the door, even as she imagined straddling Lilian.

Lord Ting plans to meet with them in secret, to calm them. She pointed with her chin to where the tube was stashed. "See, it's all in how you work your fingers."

Closing her eyes, Jie imagined Lilian's fingers walking up her belly, even as she considered Lord Ting. Known throughout the realm for his martial skill and bold leadership, he was staunchly faithful to the Emperor. The strategic location of his county helped keep the other lords around him in line, and the clan had taken keen interest in protecting him.

"Keep practicing." With a sigh, Lilian leaned in and rested her head on Jie's shoulder. Her delicate body shuddered.

What's wrong? Savoring the closeness, Jie tapped and slid her fingers in clan code on Lilian's wrist while draping her other arm over her shoulder. It was a strange occurrence in the Floating World, where an Elder Sister was supposed to comfort the House's Florets and Seedlings.

I'm tired. I don't want to do this anymore.

Jie searched Lilian's tear-filled eyes. *Why now?*

I never wanted to. Not past training and the Plucking bid.

Jie sucked on her lower lip. Using shell companies as bond holders, the clan sent many of its pretty girls to the Floating World. It usually lasted two years, not only so they could learn about pleasure, but also to hone other skills, and gather information about powerful men. Some, like Lilian, who lacked more than basic combat and stealth skills, were embedded in the prominent Houses long-term.

A tear trickled down her cheek. *I wanted to be like the Beauty, not the Steel Orchids.*

Jie nodded. Three of the most celebrated adepts in recent memory, the Beauty and the Steel Orchids had entered the Floating World as apprentices at the same time. While the Steel Orchids had remained here, the Beauty joined the Surgeon and Architect to form a team that planned and carried out the most important clan operations throughout the continent. All three had died young, twenty-one years before, but every Black Lotus Fist and initiate still idolized them.

Instead, I'm used night in, night out. Lord Ting is the worst of them all. Lilian let out a despondent sigh, one that someone listening at the door might mistake as one of pleasure.

Setting bones and stitching lacerations came easy. Attending to emotional wounds… Well, clan training fell short. Jie patted her on the back.

Lilian's mask of cheerful Blossom slipped as the tears flowed freely now. Pain and disenchantment etched worry lines into the beautiful sculpting of her face. This, after just two years of receiving men.

This might be Jie's future, as well. Despite the constant, unfulfilled urges now, it would undoubtedly grow tiring, especially compared to all the more interesting places her skills would be of use. *I'll get you reassigned. Together.* As adopted daughter of the clan's grandmaster, she might actually be able to.

If she could come up with a good reason. Lilian's stealth, combat, observation, planning, and other skills lagged behind even clan members five years her junior. The Floating World really did make best use of her assets, and her connection to Lord Ting was invaluable to the realm.

And the posting would keep her safe. No Sister had been lost here since a deadly training accident twenty years ago.

Jie stared at the messenger tube, wondering what she should do.

CHAPTER 2

Heart heavy and mind racing, Jie returned to the Florets' and Seedlings' room. Large enough to House twenty, its austerity rivaled the barracks of Black Lotus initiates. Each girl had just enough space to sleep on the reed mats, and a chest for their few personal belongings. The sooner Jie could move into her own room, the better. Or better yet, out of the Floating World altogether. With Lilian.

At the mid-morning hour, all the bedrolls lay folded at the edge of the sunlit chamber. Not including her, thirteen pretty Seedlings and Florets, aged eight to fifteen, called this room home. While they'd all ultimately earn their keep with their bodies, life in the Floating World was far better than say, the Trench. There, prostitutes controlled by the Red Dragon Triads would service dozens of men a day. At this very moment, some young girl was being exploited, and it made Jie's blood boil.

At least here, though, most of the House sisters were currently out running errands, or taking poetry and music lessons in the district's theaters. Only thirteen-year-old Ai and twelve-year-old Yin remained, playing a game of chess.

"Big Sister." They both looked up and bowed, their motions the embodiment of grace even at such a young age. In this, they'd already surpassed Jie.

"How did your lesson with Lilian go?" Yin asked. Blessed with the exquisite features of the North, she'd suffered misfortune when her father had died in a mining accident. Scouts for the Floating World had pounced like carrion birds, buying her contract from a desperate mother with three other children to feed. She'd been with Chrysanthemum Pavillion for only a year, and any description of what happened behind closed doors—and sometimes open ones—would leave her mortified.

To spare her from fainting, Jie answered simply. "Well."

"It's such an honor to learn from the Corsage. What did she teach you?" Ai's face looked bright. Coming to the House as a Seedling of eight, she'd been here long enough that a graphic description of a sex act would affect her as much as basic bookkeeping. Which was to say, anyone could fake interest.

Jie looked from Ai to Yin. What was the name of the technique again? *Squeezing Jade*? No, it had to be something a little more elegant. *Jade Thrust*? Turning to shield her hands from Yin, Jie pantomimed a motion Lilian had taught years ago and hadn't reviewed since.

Yin covered her mouth and flushed an interesting shade of red.

Brows furrowed, Ai tapped her chin. "*Duel of the Phoenix and Dragon*?"

Ah, the poetic names for something so primal. Jie nodded. Now, what was the name Lilian had used?

"So lucky." Ai let out a wistful sigh. "The way she does it...mmmm."

If Yin's original shade of red had been interesting, their language had no word to describe the new one.

With a chuckle, Jie padded over to her own chest. Making sure Ai and Yin had returned to their game, she retrieved two throwing stars from the false bottom. She adjusted her hair, pinning it up in a popular style with a sharp hairpin.

Then, she closed her eyes and thought about Lilian's message. *Lord Ting meeting with disgruntled lords, Jade Teahouse, in two days.*

Here was a chance for her and Lilian to show they could do more than trawl for information from sated men. She'd added her own missive. *Lilian wants reassignment. Let her prove herself. A hit.*

"I'm going out." She waved with a smile, as the Florets were wont to do when the Blossoms, Gardener, or Florist weren't around.

Outside of the gaudy double doors, painted with half the emblem of a chrysanthemum on each side, Jie took a deep breath of the fresh air. The entrance faced south, an auspicious position, and up to the southwest, the Iridescent Moon hung in its reliable spot in the sky, waning toward a faint third crescent. Almost ten o'clock.

She crossed the courtyard and bowed to Master Deng at the front gate, albeit with less grace than any other girl who'd spent at least a year in the Floating World.

The guard returned her greeting with a nod. "Where are you off to?"

"I'm getting a dress altered." Jie smiled at him. Though Seedlings weren't allowed out by themselves, Florets who'd earned their Houses' trust enjoyed freedom between chores and lessons. Jie's comings and goings might seem random to Deng, or any other casual observer, but coded poems known by every Black Lotus initiate and adept set a schedule of meeting times and locations.

The Floating World bustled at night with a myriad of colors and scents, but quieted by dawn, and turned into a ghost town by mid-morning. As she strolled down the narrow, stone-paved streets, a few men-at-arms nodded in greeting from the ornate brothel gates. A troupe manager stood under a theater's steeply pitched roofs and red banners and waved at her.

She returned each greeting with a polite bow appropriate for a Floret, even as her eyes assessed changes from the day before: what scent of incense burned in the Gold Orchid Shrine, the cost of opium in the dens, or the odds at the mahjong parlors.

All the buildings were packed in close, even tighter than before the fire ravaged most of the district twenty years ago. In the rush to rebuild and reap profits, nobody cared that it might happen again—save for the investors in the Chrysanthemum Pavilion and Peony Garden, who'd ensured there was plenty of space between the mansion and the walls.

Jie snorted. To think, somewhere over the years, no matter how much she'd wanted to leave, this tinder box had become home. The Floating World, named because it was where a man's dreams took flight, provided all kinds of entertainment at any budget. For Lilian, that meant letting wealthy men use her body. Maybe Jie would share the same fate, if the clan didn't deem her skilled enough for another assignment.

The heady scent of lotus incense beckoned. Turning down a secondary road, Jie paused at the Lotus Shrine, consecrated by Daoist priests long ago as a symbol for sexuality. Its lacquered black tiles, curving to give the squat, open structure the look of a lotus flower in bloom, looked dull in the morning sun. That meant a clan courier had not yet picked up messages and cleaned off a night's worth of smoke ash. A stele with a lantern at its crest rose up behind the flower, oftentimes mistaken as a symbol of male virility. Visible from anywhere in the Floating World, the lantern only lit up in a clan emergency.

With her back to Jie, a Floret in a blue dress stood with her head bowed before an ornate box which supposedly held the solid tear of the Blue Moon Goddess. She clapped once and wafted the incense smoke toward her face, in hopes of inviting the arrival of Heaven's Dew.

Jie suppressed a snort. While the rest of the realm recognized the Blue Moon as the Eye of Guanyin, Goddess of Fertility, the Daoists had their own ideas of immortality and sexuality. Tonight, lascivious men would visit and pray for an epic night in the Floating World. On occasion, Blossoms whose herbal contraception failed them would leave unwanted babies here, too, never knowing they would end up working for the Black Lotus Clan.

Finished with her prayer, the Floret turned around. She met Jie's gaze and bowed her head with well-trained grace.

Returning the bow with much less refinement, Jie approached the slat-top donation box. Using sleight of hand, she tossed one of her extra coppers and Lilian's message tube in. They clinked to the bottom, joining the coins and ingots that would help fund clan operations, as well as messages from clan sisters embedded in the other Houses. She clapped her hands together and bowed her head. If anyone happened to pass by, they'd just assume they'd seen a Floret praying for her monthly cycles to begin, and not a mythical Black Lotus Fist delivering a message.

Satisfied, she continued on her way to the meeting of clan girls. She passed through a grove of cherry trees, where folded sheets of paper were tied into knots around branches, competing with the blooms for space. While most of the notes involved prayers for good health or a spectacular night, the one Jie snagged was folded in such a way that it would tear apart in untrained hands, and contained instructions from the clan. She stuffed it into her sleeve's inner pocket.

A few blocks later, a short, thin man in a gentleman's robe stumbled out of the Jade Teahouse. He hadn't enjoyed the establishment's renowned teas, if the reek of alcohol and his wobbling feet were any indication. The burly, scowling doorman with crossed arms added yet more evidence. What had a drunkard been doing in the teahouse, at this hour?

He shook his fist at the guard and shouted a few expletives at the closing door. With no response forthcoming, he turned around and looked up and down the street. His gaze fell on her.

Feigning demureness like a good Blossom, Jie shuffled along.

The weight of the man's stare fell on her back, as heavy as his approaching footsteps.

The hairs on the back of Jie's neck stood on end. Nobody ever attacked a Blossom in the Floating World. It just didn't happen. The district's enforcers, while well-dressed and polite, could inflict a lot of pain on a man who dared lay a finger on a nonconsenting employee. The unspoken threat of retribution made the Floating World the safest place in the capital, save for the Imperial Palace.

Woe be to this fool for targeting Jie, of all people. She stopped, turned, and bowed. "May I help you, kind sir?"

He leered at her, eyes drinking her up. It might've been threatening if he weren't so small, or if Jie didn't know a thousand different ways to defend herself. A feral grin contorted his lips.

From dusk to dawn, eyes watched from all over, and a member of the Floating World enjoyed the protection of community vigilance. From mid-morning to early afternoon, however, most denizens were asleep. A scream might bring people to her rescue, but by the time they got there, it would be too late.

Her cover would be blown, city authorities—who usually left the Floating World to its own devices, as long as the businesses paid taxes to the throne—would be called in, and she'd have to explain how a waif of a girl had incapacitated a man.

He'd have to be taken care of quietly, in a secluded place. Which happened to be her specialty.

Just choke him out, apply some *yinhua* flower essence, and he'd wake up never remembering he'd seen her. Though if he'd targeted her, he'd probably assault a defenseless Blossom in the future. Maybe it'd be better to get rid of him for good. That meant calling in a clan Cleaner to dispose of the body, however, before the aforementioned authorities investigated.

Feigning fear, Jie backed up. She modulated her voice into a tremble. "Please sir, I'm just a Floret. Please don't hurt me."

He advanced, claiming the ground between them.

Pretending her skirts slowed her down, she turned and ran just fast enough to stay ahead of him. After all, if he gave up the chase, he might harm a lone Floret or Seedling running errands.

With a glance over her shoulder, she put on a burst of speed and ducked into the narrow, south-north alley between the red-roofed shrine of the Money God and the orange-tiled shrine of the Fox Spirit. A few paces in, she pulled out her bladed hairpin and clenched it between her teeth. The narrow gap allowed her to pop-vault between the tall buildings that obscured the morning sun.

Stopping twelve feet up, she shot her arms and legs out and suspended herself horizontally between the two walls. No one ever looked up; now all she had to do was wait.

And wait.

Her arms and legs started to ache. Had he given up? Or lost her in his drunken haze? She took in the scents and sounds.

Quiet. Birds chirped.

His alcohol stench drifted in from the head of the alley. Surely he couldn't be so dense as to wait there:

had she been running, she could have reached the other side. Then again, who knew what thoughts ran through an alcohol-muddled brain?

There were no man-shaped shadows at the intersection either, so he must be hiding around the corner of the western shrine's wall. Had he thought of that himself, or was it by chance? Though, unless he'd crossed the mouth of the alley when she started her ascent, she would've seen him. Her ears would've picked up his breathing.

Breaths! Shallow inhalations came from the far end of the alley. Then, a click.

She craned down and looked.

A crossbow bolt sped toward her.

She dropped as it zipped by, zigzagging between the walls, down to the pavestones. She landed in a crouch. A hooded man wearing the garb of a brothel enforcer stood at the far end of the alley, cocking a repeating crossbow. His steady stance spoke of fighting experience, likely in some foreign war where kings hired Hua mercenaries. Without aiming, he sprayed three bolts in tight arc.

The narrowness of the alley and near-impossible accuracy of the shots left no room to dodge more than one. She turned to present the side of her body, and the first brushed by her ear. She caught the second, then threw her back against the wall to avoid the third.

Why hadn't he shot another—

The drunkard—clearly not drunk—turned into the alley, a knife already coming down in a quick stab.

Crossbowman on one side, hired blade on the other. Jie ducked under the knife and slid feet-first between his legs. Spinning, she hooked his shin in the crook of her elbow and threaded her legs up and around his. Now inverted, she locked her ankles at his hip and arched back. His forward momentum dislocated his knee as he fell.

He screamed as his face hit the dirt.

Two seconds. She might have two seconds at most before the crossbowman came up and shot her in the face, point-blank, and she was still struggling with the first attacker.

Fighting through his pain, the knifeman somehow rolled over. She released him, lest he get the bright idea of slashing her Achilles tendon. Before she could get away, he was straddling her, his light weight still crushing the air out of her.

He stabbed down, but she caught his wrist in both hands. He leaned in, and her arms shook, already tired from laying her own ambush.

"Bitch." His lip curled into a sneer.

CHAPTER 3

Pinned beneath a man who'd tricked her into thinking he was a stupid drunkard looking for easy prey, Jie struggled to keep his knife out of her eye. Any second now, her trembling arms would—

His head snapped back. Blood sprayed. His muscles went slack, and Jie redirected his knife to the ground as he crumpled on top of her. His mass stifled her breath, and she struggled just to lift her head out from under him and spot the crossbowman a dozen paces away.

He looked from her to the space behind her. Though a mask hid his expression, his posture screamed of confusion. Had he shot his comrade? The crossbow trigger hadn't clicked again, had it? He turned and ran.

Closing her eyes and blowing out a breath, Jie let her head drop back down. The Floating World's twenty-year track record for clan Sister safety had almost come to an end...

"Are you all right, my sweet?" said a female voice.

Jie's eyes fluttered open, and she looked up at the source. Dressed in a simple green dress, Lilian knelt over her, her honeysuckle perfume heavy, familiar, and comforting.

What? Jie squirmed out from beneath her assailant. Her gaze flicked from Lilian to him.

A throwing spike was lodged in his eye, and he had bled all over her.

"You saved me." Jie nodded in appreciation. "That might be the best throw you've ever made."

Lilian gave a hesitant, utterly adorable bob of her head. "I never imagined you would need me to save you."

"How did you find me?"

"Coincidence." She smiled and extended a hand. "I was on my way to the gathering when I saw this man waiting on the street, with that knife."

Taking the proffered hand, Jie climbed to her feet and studied the body. Of course, there was nothing to identify him. Nothing clung under his nails, and his shoes showed no telltale clues. He'd spilled some strong rice wine onto his clothes and used it to rinse his mouth. Still, a trace of sesame-ginger marinade lingered there.

She looked up. "He knew who I was and where I would be."

"Impossible." Lilian shook her head. "The only ones who know our identities are other clan members."

Jie knelt down and checked him for other weapons. "He was waiting. He lulled me into complacency by acting like a drunk merely picking a target of opportunity."

Lilian's porcelain complexion blanched even more. "That means the crossbowman..."

"Knows about me, as well." Jie nodded. "And now also you, if they didn't already."

Still acting like a Night Blossom, Lilian covered her gasp with a delicate hand. With her other hand, though, she presented four crossbow bolts. "We need to track the crossbowman down."

"We also need to warn the others, and get word to the clan to bring a Cleaner to take care of this mess."

"I'll inform the clan." Lilian looked at the body and shuddered. Then she squared her shoulders and yanked her throwing spike from the man's face. She looked more like a Black Fist that way.

An intriguing mix of admiration and arousal shot up Jie's spine. She gave a satisfied nod. "Before you go, let me see what instructions they left for us." She withdrew the message she'd picked from the grove of trees and carefully unfolded it.

Coming up behind her, Lilian rested her chin on Jie's shoulder, her honeysuckle scent soothing after Jie's brush with death. Together, they read.

Chatter in the North of a hit on Lord Ting. He is key to stability to there. He must be protected.

Which meant that in all likelihood, the clan wouldn't reassign Lilian, Lord Ting's favorite. Jie looked over her shoulder.

Lilian's lips formed a tight line for a split second. "I didn't expect any other outcome."

"I'll think of something." Jie turned and leaned in so their foreheads touched. "Now, we need to hurry. I'll continue to the meeting. You go to the safehouse and bring more assets back to the silk market in an hour."

"As you command, Elder Sister." Lilian saluted with a fist in her palm, turned, and ran.

Jie strode to where the crossbowman had been and sniffed for any lingering smells. He'd eaten the same marinade as the dead man, and also washed his mouth out with alcohol. These men were real soldiers, and had specifically prepared to kill *her*.

It might be enough to go on. If only she could be in two places at once; then she would be able to track the crossbowman before the scent trail went cold.

Still, the other girls' safety took priority, and Jie had already wasted enough time. She took off toward the meeting place, shuffling in a nominally ladylike fashion on the streets, and dashing through alleys.

A block away from the opera house, the site of today's gathering, she stopped and took in her surroundings. Like the rest of the Floating World at this hour, it was quiet, with only the three-story wooden structure's banners fluttering in the light breeze. Then again, if these assassins had been prepared for her, they might know how to breach the theater. An image of all the girls, captured or dead, appeared unbidden in her mind. She stepped into the lookout's line of sight, flashed a hand signal, and ducked back. She peeked around the corner.

A mirror flashed twice in the sun. *All clear.*

At least on the front end. Jie extended her hands and signed, *Extra vigilance. Possible security breach.*

The mirror blinked twice again in acknowledgement.

Somewhat relieved, Jie crept through another alley that came up behind the opera house. The lookout was hidden in the usual spot, and as in front, flashed the sign that everything was all right. With no other signs of abnormal activity, she slipped in through the service door. As always, a mess of costumes and make-up paints and brushes cluttered the hallways and dressing rooms. Several dresses hung from racks, all carrying the various familiar smells of Black Lotus sisters.

Voices and thumps grew louder as she approached the stage from the back. Still nothing out of the ordinary. She let out a breath and peeked in.

Twenty-six girls, ranging in age from eight to thirty-two, were practicing Black Fist techniques in black stealth suits. Some were engaged in knife duels, while others used blindfolds to maneuver through obstacles. One crossed a narrow wooden beam while dancing through a sword form. Even in the Floating World, they met to keep their weapons, stealth, and memory skills sharp.

She hadn't needed to worry about their safety: with their knowledge of the opera house's layout, and a predetermined emergency plan that made use of hiding places and bottlenecks, an attacker would be a fool to assail the location, even if they brought a thousand men.

The only danger would be if someone wanted to burn it down—but the flames would consume most of the Floating World, as the clan training accident had, twenty years ago. Today, only her own Chrysanthemum Pavilion and the rival Peony Garden would survive, because of the space between the mansions and their walls.

That fire was never far from Jie's mind, since it had claimed all the clan's operatives in the entertainment district, including the legendary Steel Orchids. Renowned for their elegance and guile, they'd sniffed out conspiracies, rooted out traitors, and ended a rebellion before it started.

All the girls here now were heirs to that legacy, and Jie was their leader. Regardless of age or experience, they shared two things in common: pretty faces and Black Fist training. Full-fledged Blossoms brought Seedlings who were not yet allowed to leave their respective Houses on their own. Jie's chest filled with pride as she watched. She'd taught many of them at the temple, and still coached them now.

Little Wen, a precocious sixteen-year-old from the Peony Garden, disarmed nineteen-year-old Meisha's knife. She disengaged and bowed. "Elder Sister Jie."

All training came to a stop. Twenty-six sets of fists went to palms, and heads bobbed. Though all were technically sisters in the clan, Jie's position as officially adopted daughter of Clan Master Yan made her de facto leader.

She returned their salute. "Sisters, we have an emergency. Two assassins, one armed with a Repeater, targeted me specifically on my way here."

Whispers erupted.

"Where's Elder Sister Lilian?" Yuna, Little Wen's fiery new apprentice asked, flipping a knife between her fingers. She was particularly gifted, excelling at many of the clan's techniques already. She'd just been working on the No-Shadow Cut, which only a few of the clan's blademasters could execute.

"She is bringing help from the safehouse." Jie searched their eyes. Certainly none of them could betray the clan. "In the meantime, have you noticed anything out of the ordinary? Has anyone suspicious been following you?"

Heads shook.

Jie sucked on her lower lip and let it go with a pop. All of these girls, even the youngest, knew how to spot and lose tails. They'd all been trained to notice such things. "We will err on the side of caution, and assume that whoever attacked me knows who all of us are. We are all targets."

More murmuring, even though hopefully that wasn't the case. Maybe Masked Crossbowman knew only about her, the half-elf. Still, for everyone's safety... "We will change our meetings to schedule pattern three. The attacker won't know our routines; at least not for a few days. Otherwise, maintain your regular activities."

"What about now?" Wen asked.

"Lilian is reporting back to the safehouse, and will hopefully bring more assets." Jie drew a finger in a circle. "We will assume our enemy knows we are gathering here, so we will disperse now. Those who can, reconvene at the silk market, infiltration mode."

Fists went into palms, and heads bowed. They changed back into their simple dresses. In staggered groups of two or three, they left the theater from the front and back doors.

Jie waited until last, relaying commands to the lookouts, and relieving the one in front while she changed and disappeared into the alleys. Satisfied everyone was clear of the theater, Jie set off toward the silk market.

Just outside of the giant lanterns hanging from the front gates to Floating World, the silk market was erroneously considered by the capital's denizens to be part of the entertainment district. While the latter quieted from mid-morning to mid-afternoon, the silk market bustled with activity from dawn until well past dark. It was one of the few places where other women would ever rub shoulders with a Blossom.

Rows upon rows of covered stalls lined the open square. They formed a maze of virtual streets, covered by a giant red tent. Hundreds of people milled about, chatting with friends or browsing.

Others haggled with merchants over bolts of silk, cotton, and imported linen and satin, which came in all manner of designs and colors. Vendors hawked brocade shoes and the latest fashions in dresses, gowns, and robes.

Though women made up the vast majority of customers, the Floating World girls stood out with their beauty and graceful carriage, even in plain day dresses. Most servants paid them no mind, but groups of well-to-do housewives broke off in gossip, huddling together as they eyed Blossoms and Florets. The handful of noblewomen present might cast scathing glances at their husbands' possible paramours, and the reactions of their entourage of handmaidens and guards ranged from active avoidance to lecherous ogling.

While her clan sisters blended in with the crowds, Jie's tapered ears drew many eyes—just as planned, to keep the others safe. Hidden among the stares, the weight of a threatening gaze prickled the back of Jie's neck. Whether it was a run-of-the-mill serial killer, rapist, kidnapper, or an associate of the crossbowman, it was impossible to tell. If only she could find the source.

Maintain cover, she signaled while pretending to examine a godawful puce fabric. She continued on her way. Mirrors and other reflective surfaces failed to reveal her tail, and none of the other sisters indicated that they had made him, either.

There. The scent of that sesame-ginger marinade. Just a trace, but it was enough to suggest that Masked Crossbowman, or someone else who had eaten at the same place, was either nearby or had passed through within the hour.

She lifted a coin pouch off a noble's manservant on her way to one of her informants. While the slipper merchant and charm seller didn't have any worthwhile news, the jade bangle vendor did.

He flashed her a broad smile from across his table, where an array of sixty bracelets lay organized on a red silk tablecloth. He gestured to the cheapest one. "Miss Jie, I have some imperial green today."

"I was hoping you would." Jie set the stolen pouch on the table.

The vendor hefted it and nodded. "This particular piece hails from the Jinjing County. They've been trying to carve them into blossoms."

Jie picked up the bracelet as she pondered his message. Jinjing didn't have jade mines, and any reference to blossoms usually had to do with the Floating World. "The mine's owner? Or someone else?"

"The owner."

So, the Lord of Jinjing County was up to something in the Floating World. She gave a nod. "Thank you for this beautiful piece."

"Let me wrap it up for you." He plucked it from her hand, then wrapped it in a white cotton kerchief which was worth far more than the cheap stone, because of the handwritten poem on it. The writing seemed to extol spring blossoms, but was really a coded message. Back at the Chrysanthemum Pavilion she'd use the cipher to decode the poem in full, but at first glance it looked like the Lord of Jinjing was spending a lot of money in the Floating World.

With a bow of her head, she continued to check with her other sources. From the money she'd saved earlier that morning, she slipped a copper to a little pickpocket who always seemed to know the gossip. Another copper went to a beggar who had a good eye for which noble House bought what.

Little Wen and her apprentice Yuna, now both wearing pastel-pink day dresses and smelling of lavender, glided by. Wen's enviable grace made it easier to remember she was a full-fledged Blossom, despite her nickname. With a combination of hand signals and a few finger-taps on Jie's arm, she conveyed her message. *Lilian's back. No help coming.*

No help coming? Jie frowned. The message was percolating among the clan sisters, evident from the split-second looks of dismay. Not only that, the feeling of being watched disappeared.

A hush pregnant with expectation fell over the throng. People parted, opening a path.

Dan Lusha, the Corsage of the rival Peony Garden, glided through, chin held high, the epitome of elegance. Though she usually had her shiny black hair up in a style that set trends for the rest of the Floating World, today it cascaded down to her waist. She looked stunning in a plain pink day dress, even at an hour when most Blossoms were recovering from the previous night.

On one side, her Seedling wore a matching dress. No older than eight, the poor girl shivered like a cold puppy; certainly not from the temperature on this warm day. More likely it was because she had to uphold the standard of apprenticing to one of the most famous Blossoms in the Floating World—the one whose Plucking bid had held the previous record.

Though the guard at her other side wore the pastel-pink livery of the House, his gait exhibited competence. More importantly, he smelled of sesame-ginger marinade.

CHAPTER 4

While all eyes in the silk market lingered on the most celebrated Blossom, Jie evaluated her guard.

His stride, combined with eyes that roved for possible threats, spoke of competence. His height and build did not rule him out as Masked Crossbowman; although, unless he'd run off for a post-attack snack after trying to kill her, the sesame-ginger aroma was too heavy for him to be the same person.

Even so, they might be associates. Perhaps Masked Crossbowman worked for the Peony Garden, and their Gardener had specifically targeted her to maintain Lusha's record Plucking bid. It brought fame and honor to the House, after all.

If only Jie were so lucky. It would be better that way, since it would mean the clan sisters weren't in danger. It would also mean that just getting the whole deflowering thing over with would end the threat.

And, of course, there was also the possibility that the guard had just happened to eat at the same place as Masked Crossbowman, which would be helpful in tracking him down.

She slid between people and sidled up to Little Wen and Yuna. As a Blossom and Seedling of the Peony Garden, if anyone knew what management was thinking, it would be them. And clan fealty surpassed House loyalties. She tapped on her wrist. *What does your House say about my Plucking bid?*

Lusha hates you, and is constantly pouting about her record Plucking bid falling.

Would your Gardener act on it? While the Houses played a game of shifting alliances, betrayals, and backstabbing, Blossoms were tacitly off-limits to physical harm. Emotional harm was fair game, of course. Sending assassins was unheard of.

Ripples appeared on Wen's brow as she froze for a moment. *Maybe.*

What's she doing here?

Wen's lips quirked. *She's looking for a new dress for the weekend. A Tai-Ming Lord commissioned her for his son's first time.*

It was a great honor to be chosen by a First-Rank Lord's heir. *How much?*

An exorbitant amount.

Lusha was almost upon them now. Her eyes shifted to Jie for a split second before settling on Little Wen.

"Elder Sister." Wen bowed.

"Little Wen. Don't stand too close to mongrels, or you will get fleas." Lusha cast a scathing glance at Jie.

Mongrel. Clever. As if Jie hadn't heard that before.

Chatter erupted among the onlookers. Blossoms were known for duels of poetry or music, but Lusha's sharp tongue was the stuff of legends. They were about to witness an epic tongue-lashing.

Jie snorted. "You have nothing to worry about, Miss Lusha. My fleas have good taste."

A collective *ooooo* droned.

Sharp glare raking the crowd, silencing it, Lusha let out one of her famous little harrumphs. "Uncultured half-breed. Come to the Peony Garden tonight for a poetry duel, if you dare. There will be many guests on hand to celebrate Young Lord Peng Kai-Zhi's First Pollinating. His father has contracted me for ten thousand *yuan*."

Everyone in the Floating World knew about the celebration; as Corsage of the Chrysanthemum Pavilion, Lilian had received an invitation. Still, it was unusual to publicly announce a contract price, since rumors bred more interest than hard numbers. Then again, this was an ungodly amount, enough to buy a large villa in the capital. Predictably, the crowds murmured in excitement.

"And to think," Jie said, making a show of counting on her fingers, "my virginity is already worth over ten times his son's."

And more than Lusha's. The unspoken message was not lost on her, for she flushed, the ugly shade of red visible through her make-up.

Jie kept her expression innocent, as if the comment was unintentional. "As for your challenge... I'll be there."

With another huff, Lusha turned on her heel to leave. She looked over her shoulder. "See you tonight. After I'm done with you, they'll be rescinding their bids on your pock-ridden hole."

Jie feigned shock, even as her stomach churned. A poetry duel! The only rhymes Jie knew were those that clan initiates learned to memorize toxins.

Both Wen and Yuna turned and gaped.

Wen whispered, "What were you thinking? Lusha is a master poet. She'll savor making you look bad, especially if it ensures her record stands."

"It's my way in to the House to scout around, and also get a feel for your Gardener's intentions."

Pouting in the cutest way, Wen squeezed her hand. "I could've done that, without risking your Plucking bid."

Jie sucked on her lower lip. Wealthy men's obsession with virginity—their own and their partners'—just made them willing dupes over something whose value was based in perception. Her Plucking bid would fund clan operations for a year. And, if she had to admit it to herself, she was proud of it: utterly lacking in a Floating World Blossom's renowned grace, she still drew higher bids than the most celebrated Night Blossom of them all.

Right now, though, Wen's wounded expression took precedence. Jie smiled at her. "I need you to do something more important: her guard. Find out where he ate."

"Mister Meng?" Wen gave a perplexed rise of her eyebrow.

"His breath. It smelled the same as Masked Crossbowman. A sesame-ginger marinade. Lusha's breath didn't smell the same, so it isn't something she ate at your House."

Yuna's mouth formed a pretty circle. "Your nose never ceases to amaze me."

From what Jie could tell, full humans had poor vision and senses of smell. It was a wonder they'd lasted so long. "Can you find out?"

Wen gave an enthusiastic nod. "I'll ask him for a recommendation when he gets back to the House."

No sooner did Wen and Yuna head off then Meisha approached. The older Blossom tapped on Jie's wrist as she passed. *No Cleaner. No reinforcements.*

Jie's gut clenched. No Cleaner meant there was a dead body lying in an alley, waiting to be found. No reinforcements from the clan meant they were on their own. No doubt, this second message would be passed through taps and finger-brushes among all the sisters by now. She scanned the crowds, backtracking from Meisha to the other clan members.

Some of the younger ones' expressions were contorted in dismay, but by and large, they'd taken the bad news in stride. Hopefully, the assassin had been sent by the Peony Garden to specifically target Jie, and the others weren't at risk.

At the end of the message relay, she found Lilian, who gave her an apologetic nod.

Jie bowed as a junior should to a senior Blossom. "I couldn't find the color you wanted."

"Then we must hasten back for lessons." Lilian beckoned.

As she followed Lilian back toward the Floating World, Jie passed one last message to one of the sisters. *Resume regular activities. Maintain vigilance. Watch for light atop the Lotus Shrine.*

Hopefully, that would reassure them, even if Jie didn't feel much better.

Once they passed the gates and into the quiet of the late-morning Floating World, Jie whispered, "Why no clan support?"

Lilian sighed. "Only one brother was at the safe house. The Emperor stayed an extra day at the summer villa, so all extra hands are there to protect him. The only ones left in the city are in critical areas."

Jie's chest tightened. As if the Floating World wasn't the most important nexus of information, and the sisters gathering it weren't critical. "We need to dispose of the body before anyone finds it."

"We do?" Lilian's face turned an interesting shade of green. They'd all dissected cadavers as children, and if memory served, she'd nearly vomited every class. Apparently, little had changed. It might be that much harder to get her reassigned.

"Come on. It will cause quite the stir, and the local authorities won't know what to make of his fatal wound." Jie grinned. "It was a great throw."

"You already said so." Lilian flashed her crooked smile, which had enchanted many a wealthy patron. "But I don't mind you repeating it."

Stomach erupting in butterflies, Jie leaned in and rested her head on Lilian's shoulder. "It was a great shot."

Lilian squeezed her hand. To any prying eyes, it would look like the sisterly affection between Night Blossoms.

There was no activity around the opening to the alley; a good sign. Jie turned the corner.

And skidded to a stop.

The body was gone, along with all trace of the attack.

She turned to Lilian. "You said there was no Cleaner?"

Scanning the area, Lilian gave a tentative nod. "If not us, then who?"

"Masked Crossbowman or his friends." Jie knelt over the spot where the man had fallen and set her hand on the pavestones. They were a fraction warmer than those in the surrounding area, so it couldn't have been long. "He was quite dead, so he couldn't have walked off by himself. That means—"

"They didn't want his body found, either."

On second glance, though the pavestones looked clean, thin scuff marks from shoes and displaced grit suggested that whoever it was had dragged the body deeper into the alley. Jie followed the faint trail to where it stopped, about halfway down.

"What are you doing?" Lilian asked.

"A trail."

Lilian knelt and stared at the ground. "Where?"

Pointing, Jie sniffed the air. The coppery tang of blood still hung here, in minute traces. "They covered the wound; otherwise there'd be a blood trail, or a sign that they'd cleaned up afterwards."

Lilian looked up the shrine walls on either side, each rising nearly fifteen feet. "They somehow lifted him up and over?"

That would explain why the trail stopped there, with no body. Still, it would take a lot of effort to bring him up that high. Jie pop-vaulted to the top and looked over the side of each wall. Still no sign of the body. She came down and sniffed again. The scent of blood had thinned even more.

"Any clues?" Lilian asked.

Shaking her head, Jie sniffed around, but the scent didn't grow any stronger. "For now, our only lead is the guard at the Peony Garden."

Lilian's head rose and fell in slow bobs. "What do we do now?"

"I need your help with improvised poetry."

"Whatever for?" Lilian's brow furrowed.

Jie grinned. "I am going with you to the Peony Garden's soirée tonight. I accepted a poetry duel with Lusha."

"You did what?" Lilian blanched. "She's the most celebrated poet in the Floating World in a generation."

"Then you can't tell the Gardener or Florist that's why I'm going with you."

CHAPTER 5

"Absolutely not." Shaking her head so hard it might fall off, the Gardener stood up from her desk and slapped her palm on its shiny surface. Looking more like a Black Lotus trainer than a brothel owner, she glared from Jie to Lilian and back again.

Behind her stood Florist Wei, gaze sympathetic. She folded her hands into the long sleeves of her green dress.

Despite Jie's best efforts to keep her impromptu invitation to the Peony Garden secret, rumors in the Floating World sprouted faster than toxic mushrooms after a spring rain. Gardener Ju, a woman of middling years whose charm and talents—and supposedly an exceptionally limber body— still drew Hummingbirds to her bed, had summoned Jie and Lilian to her office just as the House's mid-afternoon preparations had begun.

Jie bowed her head. “Please, Gardener. I can’t back down. I’d lose face.”

“Not as much as when Lusha humiliates you.” The Gardener’s eyes sharpened like blades. “You’ve been here for six years, and still have less grace and propriety than a second-year Seedling.”

Bowing low, Jie stewed. It wasn’t as though she couldn’t learn all the inane rituals. It just wasn’t worth the effort. Not when she’d eventually leave the Floating World and make use of her real skills.

The Gardener rounded her desk, subtly limping from an old injury to her left leg. She harrumphed. “You’d be worthless, if not for your exotic face and pointed ears.”

Behind her, the Florist gave a subtle shake of her head. How ironic that it was an accountant who had the most warmth among the seniors in this House.

The Gardener’s ire shifted to Lilian. “And you: not only allowing her, but trying to hide it.”

“I’m sorry.” Lilian bowed low.

The Gardener turned back to Jie, teeth gritted. “Many wealthy patrons will be there tonight, including three of your highest bidders. If you lose badly, they’ll be well within their rights to rescind their bids. That would be bad for our House, and bad for your contract holder.”

Jie suppressed a smirk. The Gardener couldn't care less about her contract holder, supposedly a broker of orphan girls, but really a shell company for the Black Lotus Clan. Her concern was her cut of the Plucking bid, part of the payment for Jie's training. The clan, on the other hand... While it certainly stood to lose a pretty copper *fen*, the amount didn't begin to compare to the financial benefits of imperial patronage.

Still, every Floret cared about her Plucking bid, and Jie chastised her own vanity for feeling the same. She lowered her bow another several degrees. "I'm sorry, Gardener. I wasn't thinking of the consequences."

"It's time you learned." The Gardener searched her eyes. "Once you finish your afternoon chores, you will be confined to Lilian's room tonight, with a guard posted outside the door. His overtime pay will come from your bond."

Jie held her bow, if only to keep her smile hidden. No doubt, the Gardener assumed that with Lilian's room on the third floor, as far from the main entrance as possible, Jie had no way of sneaking out. Which she would, since the safety of her clan sisters preempted any concern about risks to her Plucking bid. "As you command, Gardener."

With a huff, the Gardener sat back down and returned to writing a letter.

The Florist cleared her throat. “Gardener, may they go?”

Not looking up, the Gardener waved a dismissive hand.

The Florist gave them a sympathetic look. “Off you go.”

Coming out of her bow, Jie exchanged glances with Lilian and departed.

Lilian flashed hand signals. *Is there anything I can do to convince you not to go?*

Of course not. Jie grinned.

She followed Lilian back to her room. While Lilian freshened up for the soirée at the Peony Garden, Jie decoded the poem the jade vendor had given her, using a cipher made just for him. Since he’d written a poem, the message contained several ambiguities; but the gist was that the Lord of Jinjing had dropped an exorbitant amount of money in many of the Houses over the last several months.

Not sure of what to make of it, other than his seed likely going dry, Jie went about her afternoon. Today it was her turn to clean and set up the spacious common room, which vaulted three stories up with mezzanines overlooking it. While most of the Seedlings and Florets despised the messy work, it was not all that different from processing a crime scene. Memories of which wealthy merchant or lord sat where, ate what, and saw whom, all formed a tapestry of information.

Last night, Lord Ting had sat in front of the right-hand side of the stage, his favorite spot, entertaining a minor lord. Perhaps trying to assuage his concerns about the empire? So dashing and formidable, he looked like a hero of old next to the other lord. Beloved by the imperial court. Adored by the populace. If only the common folk knew what he enjoyed behind closed doors.

Jie had served them, ostensibly to attract more bids on her virginity, but really to eavesdrop. They'd quieted as soon as she approached, despite the Floating World convention that anything that happened here, stayed here.

Nonetheless, Lilian had gathered significant damning information over the months: stockpiling of weapons, unapproved saltpeter mines, suspicious transactions. The Emperor had yet to order any action, hoping Lord Ting could solve the problem peaceably.

Now working where Lord Ting had sat, Jie looked up to the second-floor mezzanine. Lilian had stood there, beckoning him. His rosewood chair's angle in relation to the matching round table suggested he'd been in a hurry to leave. Apparently, a tumble between the sheets took precedence over talking an underling out of treason.

He wouldn't come calling tonight; not with Lilian at the Peony Garden.

Along with Jie, who'd find a way to slip the Gardener's watchful eye.

***

Jie studied the dwarf-made padlock, considering. Though the first-floor window shutters had simple hook locks, the second and third floors had none. The Gardener must've been quite concerned about Jie trying to escape to not only to lock this shutter, but also use an expensive device usually reserved for the most valuable treasures. It was almost flattering to be thought of as such.

Maybe it was meant as a warning; or perhaps punishment. Otherwise, it bordered on overkill. The Gardener didn't know Jie could scale the walls, after all. She also didn't know that elf ears could hear the tumblers in the lock.

Jie set to work, turning the combination at each click. Six turns and ten seconds later, it yielded with a snick.

She chuckled to herself. If the Chrysanthemum Pavilion had known about her true identity, the Gardener would've had Jie naked and chained. It certainly wouldn't be the first time that had happened to a Blossom in the House, though under very different circumstances.

Time to pick something out to wear. Lilian had numerous beautiful gowns, many gifts from Hummingbirds. Her pink dress with embroidered doves would suggest innocence, and possibly drive up bids. With a grin, Jie went to Lilian's closet and slid open the door.

Empty.

Her brow furrowed. The Gardener had taken beyond extraordinary precautions but she still underestimated Jie.

Channeling her Inner Steel Orchid, she lifted the carpet, revealing the floorboard door to a secret compartment. Inside, she found Lilian's stealth suit, a curved dagger, and several throwing spikes and stars. In a segmented compartment lay several vials of intoxicants, packed carelessly close to the three crossbow bolts retrieved from earlier today as evidence; unmistakable from Jie's own scent on the one she'd caught. Given Lord Ting's penchant for rough play, a jolt in the wrong place could crack the vials.

Jie banished the thought of Lilian taming Lord Ting with her body. She withdrew the stealth suit. The stretchy material would've been skin-tight but flexible on Lilian's larger frame, allowing freedom of motion without the risk of snagging a loose sleeve, or a droopy pant leg knocking something over. Even with Jie's smaller build, the clothes fit snugly. If the common folk believed that the Black Fists were more than boogiemen that stole disobedient children, the stealth suit embellished Lilian's curves so much that her patrons might want her to roleplay Naughty Assassin in it. *Seduce the Assassin Before She Kills You*, they'd call it.

Wearing Lilian's larger Black Fist shoes, with the big toe separated from the others, she tiptoed to the door and listened. The guard's breathing had slowed, perhaps to the point of dozing off. The sound of revelry carried on, though quieter than on most nights, given that everyone who was anyone would be attending the party at the Peony Garden. With free time on her hands, maybe the Gardener would check on her, maybe not. There was no way to prepare for that possibility.

Satisfied she could do no more to hide her tracks, Jie went to the window and looked. The chamber overlooked the capital's southeast reservoir, which reflected the red lanterns hanging above the Floating World's perimeter moat. It left the wall in darkness.

Yet another House guard patrolled the courtyard below. Maybe he was there to prevent intruders from climbing through a first-floor window, or attempting to go in through the door to the kitchens, but that wasn't standard procedure on a regular night.

And given that tonight would be slower than usual because of the festivities at the Peony Garden, it meant the Gardener had placed the guard there for her.

She turned to the last exit from the room: the fireplace. Only three rooms in the entire mansion had this rare architectural feature from the land of the fair-skinned: Lilian, as preeminent Blossom, had one; and right below, the Gardener's own room. On the first floor, the common room's hearth backed up to the kitchens' ovens. All four shared the same flue network, merging close to the roof.

With the ovens raging at full blast, those last three feet risked burns and smoke inhalation, and guaranteed soot and ash in every pore.

Still, it provided the easiest way out, and some ashes over her naturally pale complexion would help her move through the night. She took Lilian's pillow case and tore it to cover her hands, and her mouth and nose. It smelled like Lilian's hair, all honeysuckle and honey.

Then she started her climb. Past the wind shelf, the width of the first section of flue forced her to wriggle up, hands close to her body. At the flue junction, she reached up and tested the bricks.

Hot, but not scalding. She might have two seconds to clear this last section without burning her palms through the remains of Lilian's pillowcase. She took a deep breath, grabbed the hot ridge where the flues merged, and propelled herself up. Black smoke made it difficult to see. Her feet found purchase on the ridge, and she jumped, shooting her hands and feet out to suspend herself in the larger flue. The bricks heated her palms as she spider-climbed to the top. With a last burst of energy, she gripped the burning rim of the chimney, pulled herself out, and flipped over on to the tiles.

Her feet slipped on the steep pitch, the ash on the too-large shoes providing poor traction on slick tiles. She slid, much too fast, her body going over the eaves. At the last second, she shook off her improvised hand wraps and grabbed hold of the edge.

She'd almost become a splatter of half-elf in the courtyard below.

Heart racing, she blew out a breath and swung over to the closest window shutters. Her toes found the narrow ledge, and she reached under the eaves and pulled herself over. After the initial scare, the descent was child's play. She and Lilian had done this so many times that finding the hand and footholds in the planks, window sills, and awning tiles came easily.

Her feet landed on the pavestones without a sound. With her elf vision adjusting to the darkness and transforming the world into hues of grey-green, she dashed over to the compound walls, climbed over, and took shadowed back alleys to the Peony Garden. Chrysanthemum Pavillion's main rival in the Floating World, it lay just a block away. Their very layouts were similar, since they'd been designed by the same architect.

Which meant Jie might be able to get in and out without ever having to confront Lusha in a poetry duel.

CHAPTER 6

Jie stood toward the rear of the Peony Garden, a near-exact replica of the Chrysanthemum Pavilion. Given the hour and the festivities, there'd be no easy insertion points. The Florist's and Gardener's windows would certainly be locked from the inside, as would most of the other first-floor windows.

Yuna would be in the trainee room, but getting her attention risked waking the other Seedlings. Instead, Jie climbed over the walls, then up to the red-tiled awning on the second floor. There, she crept along, checking the other windows. Most stood unshuttered to let in the cool night air. In some rooms, Florets still fussed with their Blossoms' jewelry, hair, and make-up. From the giggling and grunting in a few others, some Blossoms had already left the party to bring impatient Hummingbirds back to their rooms.

Jie looked up at the third-floor windows. With her arms so exhausted, it wasn't worth the risk of finding yet more occupied rooms. She climbed down and proceeded to the kitchens.

As expected, the back door lay ajar and the kitchens buzzed with activity, like the Black Lotus Temple's training Hall of Darting Daggers. Chefs' apprentices prepped meats and vegetables, while higher-ups stir-fried, braised, and steamed delicacies fit for a great lord. Florets scurried to take small plates of snacks, only to transform into the embodiment of beauty as they passed through the doors to the common room.

Swallowing down a pit of jealousy, Jie entered. She threaded through the bustle, always using someone's back as cover, twisting or ducking to avoid the gaze of anyone who happened to look up from their work. She reached the open side door and slipped through into a side yard.

As in the Chrysanthemum Pavilion, the little courtyard provided easy servant access to the bathhouses. She kept to the shrubs lining the mansion, pausing behind each of the two cherry blossom trees before coming to the servants' door.

No sounds came from within, as would be expected at this hour. She opened the door and peeked in. Partially shuttered light-bauble lamps hung between three sliding doors on either side of the hall, shedding enough light for her vision to return to normal. The double doors at the far end muffled the festive sounds from the common room. If someone happened to open the door…

Jie zigzagged over the nightingale floors and came to the closest door. Confirming no one dallied inside, she slid it open and ducked in.

Warm, humid steam filled her lungs, percolating off a central wooden tub set into the wood floors. A polite half-elf would've scrubbed herself clean outside of the tub, using the basins on the floor and the towels in the cubbies. Time being of the essence, she stripped off the filthy stealth suit and slipped into the bath.

The tepid water nearly made her yelp. Though Black Lotus training included meditating under freezing waterfalls, many years had passed since Jie had done so. Heated by copper pipes which ran under the mansion from the central hearth, the baths had yet to reach optimal temperature.

A wave of ash and grit floated out from her sooty body, ruining the water for others. She rinsed out her hair and scrubbed her skin, all the while bemoaning her flat body. With very few half-elves mentioned in history to use an example, who knew when she'd fill out? Until then, she was cursed to remain in the Floating World, working as a Floret.

Satisfied she'd washed the evidence of her chimney escapades away, Jie climbed out, dried herself off, and donned one of the white silk bathrobes hanging from a hook above the cubbies. She tied her hair up and secured it with a bladed hairpin and lockpicks. To prevent some poor Seedling or Floret from receiving a browbeating for the dirty water, Jie unplugged the stopper—they came loose often during Hummingbirds' exuberant play.

She then removed the light baubles from the lamps and wrapped them in the stealth suit, which she in turn folded into the towel. With a quick look to see that the scene was otherwise undisturbed, she crept back into the hallway and out into the yard.

Slipping into Lilian's shoes, Jie glided around the outside of the bathhouse and into a wider courtyard. On the veranda off of the mansion, partially shuttered light baubles illuminated several distinguished-looking men cavorting with Blossoms. The ladies covered obligatory giggles at bad jokes with their dainty hands.

The white robe would make it difficult to sneak past them unseen, so Jie turned back. Fingers and toes finding handholds in the bathhouse's planks, she wormed her way up to the roof. Using the pitch of the roof to keep herself hidden from the veranda and balconies, she worked her way back to the central mansion.

A window overlooked the bathhouse roof, a line of light shining between the shutters. Testing the hinges to make sure they were well-oiled, Jie opened one of the leaves a crack and peeked in. No people or shadows moved, and the only the sounds came from the party below. She opened it just wide enough for her slight build and climbed in.

Rosewood chairs flanked a decorative table on a round wool carpet. A large bed with a matching rosewood frame occupied the east wall, while brush paintings hung on the walls. The lack of Dragonscribe magic in them, and the spring motifs in the art, suggested the room belonged to a newer Blossom.

Jie crept over to the dressing niche and looked in a mirror standing on a make-up table. Indeed, compared to the celebrated Corsages of the Floating World, elf-blood made her exotic, unique: dark brown hair instead of black, a sharper nose, larger eyes, and those tapered ears. A clan elder had once said, *The wealthiest men in the realm will seek her out. Her Plucking bid alone will fund clan operations for a year, and even after, they'll line up for the chance to be next.*

She sighed. Like Lilian, she'd be stuck in the Floating World, gathering information and making money for the clan while lying on her back. Maybe it was time to practice the renowned grace of the Blossoms.

Shaking the thought out of her head, she turned her attention to the paper lodged into the mirror frames. The self-affirmations, notes on Hummingbird kinks, and a cosmetics shopping list indicated the room belonged to Namei, a pretty girl from the coast.

Jie's gaze settled on a bar where several gowns hung. All consisted of inner and outer gowns that embellished cleavage and exposed long legs—assets that the Heavens had yet to bless her with, and none suited a Floret trying to project innocence. Little Wen, however, might still have the perfect dress for the occasion.

Jie went to the door and slid it open enough to poke her head through. As in the Chrysanthemum Pavilion, the mezzanine overlooking the common room ran around the perimeter of the second floor, with doors to the Blossom's rooms. Music from the four-stringed *pipa* and eighteen-stringed *guzheng* percolated up from below.

This room lay up and to the right of the stage, and a tall man standing by the balcony blocked her from view. Wearing fine blue silk robes, he smelled of oiled steel. He held his thumbs and forefingers to form a rectangle, as if framing a picture. Maybe he was an artist? She followed his line of sight to the corner of the stage, where a Peony Garden Floret was serving drinks to a pair of wealthy-looking merchants while they ogled her.

If this man was an artist, he must've been influenced by the trends among the fair-skinned, since this particular scene was so...mundane. *Desperate Men*, she'd name it. If the opportunity presented itself, she'd be sure to get a look at his face.

She started to recede back to the wall, but paused. Lilian approached the two merchants in the corner and bowed with the grace of a phoenix. Jie remained transfixed. No matter how many times she'd watched Lilian at the Chrysanthemum Pavilion, her elegance never ceased to evoke both envy and arousal. With a hard swallow, she backed away.

Some Blossoms loitered with Hummingbirds along the mezzanine railing, giggling and pointing. With their backs to the doors, Jie stayed close to the wall and slunk behind them, turned a corner, and ducked into Little Wen's room.

The partially shuttered light-bauble lamp shed a dim light over a room furnished much like the other. Jie went to the bed and stashed Lilian's stealth suit and shoes underneath, then took one of the light baubles before going to the dressing niche. Deep within one of the drawers, she found the dress that had contributed to Wen's considerable Plucking bid, from a time when her build was similar to Jie's now.

Green silk with embroidered yellow and white flowers, the one-piece's neckline emphasized the nape, top of the shoulder blades, and collarbones. Hanging sleeves would slide into the crook of a bent elbow, embellishing willowy arms, and the single slit could expose just enough leg to tantalize. Jie slipped into it, then borrowed some of Wen's rouge to give her cheeks a pink tint. With a quick look in the mirror, Jie pinned her hair in a way that concealed her ears. She stashed the light bauble in her undergarments.

Now, it became a matter of sneaking down to the common room without being seen, in a dress that was meant to be seen; then finding an opportunity to investigate the Florist's and Gardener's offices for evidence of a plot against her or the clan.

Again using the Blossoms and guests along the railing as cover, Jie worked her way over to one of the stairwells and hurried down. It opened into a dimly lit hall between the common room and veranda, which also led to an office. Waiting for a drunk man on the arm of a Blossom to stumble past, she turned out of the stairwell. Not having time to find the joists in the nightingale floor, she stepped in time with the amorous couple in the opposite direction, and reached the office door.

A dwarf-made lock was set in the door, openable with the right key. The devices had flooded the market in the last ten years with increased trade with the East, but proved only a little harder to pick than the local padlocks. Not only that, a passerby wouldn't even notice it had been breached. It yielded to her lockpicks, and she slipped into the dark room.

Her elf vision took over, casting the office in hues of green and grey. With shelves of ledgers and an abacus, this had to be the Florist's office. While it was tempting to find out Lusha's actual Plucking bid, recent transactions would provide more insight into possible assassin hires. She pulled out the one with the most recent label. A folded sheet of paper slipped from between its pages, and Jie snatched it out of the air without a sound. Opening her mouth, she secured the light bauble between her teeth. She looked at the ledger's binding and found the subtle gap between pages where the sheet had slipped from.

She opened to that spot and found a record of the most current expenditures. Contracting a murder could cost upwards of a thousand gold *yuan*, so she looked first to the largest receivables. Three stood out, all listed as going toward Young Lord Peng's

First Pollinating. Curiously, not all came from Lord Peng, though it was plausible the three companies who had paid the balance had received some favor in return. A quick skim over the past hundred days of transactions showed no totals that would add up to hiring an assassin.

Still, there was a familiar scent. She sniffed. The sesame-ginger marinade! She snuffled more, no doubt looking more like a pig searching for truffles than a Floret trying to attract bids. The minute traces came from...the folded sheet of paper.

She unfolded it and scanned. The script looked graceful and feminine.

The common room must be set up exactly like—

Laughing and chirping footsteps grew louder in the hall, coming to a stop at the door. The handle jiggled.

"It's unlocked," said a male voice.

CHAPTER 7

Standing by the desk in the Florist's office, Jie snatched up the ledger and returned it to its shelf, letter and all. She stashed the light bauble in her mouth and ducked under the table just as the door opened.

Two sets of legs staggered in, visible from under the writing table: one male in dark silk robes, the other the willowy limbs of a Night Blossom. They closed the door to a crack, allowing a blade of light in.

The couple approached, the male's feet pointed forward, the female's shuffling back as she giggled.

"I've always wanted to do it on a table," he said.

"We can't, my Lord." The voice was familiar: Meina, from the Peony Garden, a pretty but not-so-smart girl. "Not in the Florist's office. Come back to my room."

Yes, go back to your room. Jie gritted her teeth. The desk screeched on the floor as he pressed the girl into it, providing an up-close look at the middle of their thighs. As sturdy as it looked, the table probably wasn't built to support one person, let alone two in the throes of passion.

The woman squealed as her feet left the floor. She landed on the desk, which creaked in protest. His robe parted and his pants and undergarments dropped to his ankles. He grunted, and she gasped.

As part of her training, Jie had witnessed coupling more times than a child's abacus could calculate, from straightforward positions to those a yogi from the lands of the bronze-skinned would envy. It was neither titillating nor disgusting, just a means to an end. Right now, though, it might mean her end—either from a table collapsing on her, or their noise drawing someone in.

Angling herself to fit in the space between the table's legs and his, Jie slipped through. With the man preoccupied, she stayed low out of the Blossom's line of sight and darted through the space in the door. She gained her feet, smoothed the dress out, and hurried toward the common room.

She paused at the archway and looked.

Up on the balcony across from her, the artist was gone. In his place stood another man, peering at something on Jie's side of the room. She followed his gaze.

He was looking at the same corner by the stage, but this time several men wearing the livery of Lord Ting stood there. They gazed at Peony Garden Blossoms who were dancing sensually on stage to a quartet of stringed instruments. Her eyes shifted to the source of the music, a space in front of the stage. The famous Master Ding Meihui's fingers swam over her *pipa* strings, so mesmerizing that it was hard to tell if she created the music, or the music moved her fingers. Rumor had it she was close to rediscovering the lost magic of Dragon Songs, which had helped free mankind from the Tivari ages ago. Lord Peng must've paid a handsome sum; she usually performed for the Emperor himself, and supposedly even taught eight-year-old Princess Kaiya.

Jie's gaze shifted to the left of the musicians, where Dan Lusha sat in Young Lord Peng Kai-Zhi's lap, giggling like a girl ten years younger. Indeed, her heavy make-up almost accomplished that effect, even if the low cut of her white inner gown exposed far more than it hid, and the translucent outer gown left nothing it covered to the imagination. Peng Kai-Zhi was flushed red, whether from alcohol or embarrassment, it was hard to tell; but at just sixteen, he otherwise looked every part the heir to his province in his formal robes. Clan members embedded in the palace reported that his younger brother, Kai-Long, was adored by the Emperor—their maternal uncle—and that he helped keep an eye on Princess Kaiya.

Bowing lords and ministers all approached and toasted him, while prominent Blossoms of all the major Houses introduced themselves with dainty bows. Lilian, dressed in a gown nearly as revealing as Lusha's, scanned the room as she mingled with the other Blossoms, her Black Fist-trained eyes taking in every detail without actually appearing to.

Jie sucked on her lower lip. This would be her future life—perhaps for decades, given the youthful effect of elf blood—if she didn't prove herself or get murdered over her virginity first. For now, though, she had to confirm she was the Peony Garden's only target.

The original plan had been to mingle with the guests, and perhaps eavesdrop on the Florist, until an opportunity presented itself to break away and investigate the offices. Now, with one office down, maybe there was a safer option: all she had to do was make it through the festivities and to the opposite hall without being noticed.

Checking to ensure her hair still covered the tips of her ears, she used a walking man as cover to cross a quarter of the room. She froze in a dead space, surrounded by backs. That sesame-ginger smell was emanating from somewhere in the room. Unfortunately, the same milling bodies that kept her hidden also prevented her from getting a good visual scan.

She swept up a porcelain tray with rice wine cups from a table and continued as if she were one of the House Florets, until she ducked behind yet another man in dark blue silk. The smell of oiled steel. The artist from the balcony.

Jie shot a glance up to the mezzanine corner. The man who'd been there moments before was gone, replaced by another man in crimson livery. What was it about that spot? That was a question for later, because here was a chance to see Artist's face. She angled the tray so that his face reflected in a cup of rice wine.

Given the position of the lights, a scar across his forehead was all that distinguished him. He started to turn.

Jie ducked away, continuing toward the opposite archway. It was too easy. The scent grew stronger. Just another few—

"You!" A middle-aged patron of the Chrysanthemum Pavillion waved at her from a table ahead to the left. Deputy Xun from the Ministry of

War. "You're the half-elf Floret from the Chrysanthemum Pavilion! Jie, was it?"

Shit. Jie pretended she hadn't heard while continuing on her way. He reached for her as she passed, but she deftly avoided his hand by turning and setting the tray down on a nearby table. The sesame-ginger smell diffused.

And now, more eyes fell on her. Excited whispers broke out.

"It's Ju Jie!"

"I bid thirty thousand yuan on her virginity."

"She's almost too awkward for a Blossom, but that face!"

A large body stepped in front of her; easy enough to avoid, but doing so would raise questions.

Jie stopped and looked up.

Minister Li from the Imperial Treasury met her eye. Using his huge frame, he angled himself, boxing her against a wall. "So, you are the Chrysanthemum Pavilion's famous half-elf."

Men like this prowled the Floating World, using their size to project dominance over Blossoms and Florets alike. Every female, from Sprout to Gardener, had endured it. Despite their training to maintain calm while feigning demureness, most feared the experience.

Most, but not embedded Black Lotus Fists. Certainly not Jie. There were a dozen different ways to slip out of this trap, and even more to mete out pain or permanent injury. Still, clan training in keeping a clear head under duress melded perfectly with Floating World skills in manipulating fragile male psyches. Jie cast her gaze down and trembled. "Yes, Master."

In an audacious move, he lifted her chin with a finger. His leer roved over her, making her feel dirtier than after the trip up the chimney. "What is your Plucking bid up to? I would like to make a bid."

"I'm sorry, only my Gardener and Florist know. You will have to speak with them."

"I'd like to speak to *you*." His breath burned hot on her neck as he leaned in.

Her shudder this time might not have been entirely acting. Her arms and legs froze, and she couldn't form a coherent thought.

A hand clamped around hers.

Fighting reflexes took over, jolting Jie out of her fear. She turned her hand over and started twisting into a wrist lock.

Her captor's hand reacted smoothly, avoiding the technique with practiced skill. "Minister Li, thank you for finding my Little Sister."

Jie looked at the hand on hers. The dorsal side was delicate and smooth, belying the callouses on the palm and fingers. She followed a silk-clad arm up and met Lilian's stern gaze.

"Come along now, Little Jie." Lilian's voice sounded gentle, even as the swipes and taps of her finger on the back of Jie's hand said otherwise. Sometimes it was a good thing their clan's non-verbal communication didn't include expletives. *What are you doing here*?

"Thank you for your interest, Master." Jie bowed, while tapping back, *Scouting*.

Minister Li stared at the both of them, eyes wide and mouth moving, but no words coming out.

"Come, Little Jie." Lilian gave her a tug toward the entrance. *Too big a risk. We need to get you out before Lusha sees you.*

"Look what—I mean, *who* we have here!" Lusha's soft, melodious voice managed to boom over the throng. "I didn't see Little Ju Jie from the Chrysanthemum Pavilion. Lilian said you had later declined the invitation. Come, pay respects to Young Lord Peng."

Conversation quieted to a low murmur. Heads looked from the couple of honor to Jie, and the crowds parted to form an aisle between them.

Lusha beckoned with a graceful wave of her hand.

Jie sucked on her lower lip. Had everything gone perfectly, she would've been in and out without ever having to engage in a poetry duel.

"I'm sorry, Miss Lusha." Lilian bowed low. "My Little Sister is dizzy from all the guests. I was going to take her out for some fresh air."

The House Gardener, wearing a blue gown with a white inner dress, stepped into view. She beckoned to someone near the entrance. "Oh, it is much too cold outside. We don't want you freezing."

Never mind that it wasn't cold. House guards took up position at the entrance and the doors to the veranda. It wouldn't be hard to make it by them, but again, it would raise questions about how a Floret had such talents.

"I will assign one of our men to escort you to the conservatory. Plenty of fresh air, with all the open windows. Over here, Shixian."

Making it no warmer than outside, so temperature clearly wasn't the Gardener's concern. Her feral grin suggested ill intentions. She now hooked her hands into the crook of a handsome young man's elbow and pulled him into the aisle through the crowds.

Shixian was his name, apparently, and he was staring straight at her.

Then again, so was everyone else.

Shixian approached, the scent of rust growing stronger. His swishing robes didn't match the livery of the other House guards.

And he moved like a trained killer.

Like Masked Crossbowman.

CHAPTER 8

Jie took an involuntary step back as the Peony Garden guard, Shixian, approached. She tapped a message onto Lilian's arm as she pulled her back. *He's the one from this morning.*

Lilian looked down at her, brow creased. *Are you sure?* she mouthed.

Was she? Jie studied the tall man. It was hard to tell, since he wasn't advancing and retreating with a repeating crossbow in hand. He walked with purpose, though he didn't seem to have any weapons. Still, all it would take was deft sleight of hand to slip any number of poisons into Jie's drink. And of course, there were contact toxins.

Jie took a deep breath. It wouldn't be the first, and certainly not the last time someone tried to kill her. She still had Lilian, and...her eyes found Little Wen, the only other Black Lotus member among all the people present.

Lines of worry were etched into her pretty features. She signed, *Not a House guard. Get out.*

Brushing her hair behind her ears, Jie signaled with a combination of finger motions and eye expressions. *I will handle. Maintain line of sight.*

Shixian came closer. He had a strong jaw, and large eyes embellished by a high nose bridge and sculpted brow. Unlike most of the lechers in attendance, he was fresh, handsome. He beamed like a ray of sun stabbing through storm clouds.

Her pulse quickened against her better judgement.

He reached her and bowed. "Miss Jie."

"Mister Shixian." She returned his salute, deftly dodging his attempt to brush up against her.

His forehead scrunched up for a split second before he extended a hand toward the conservatory. As in the Chrysanthemum Pavillion, it lay through the archway to the other office. They passed through, crossed the hallway, and went under another arch. A cool—but not cold—breeze greeted her as they stepped into a long room lined with open windows. Empty save for a few rosewood chairs, it mirrored the veranda on the other side. Behind them, guards barred the way to any others. Lilian craned to keep an eye on them.

Well, if they wanted to kill Jie with no witnesses, they'd made a mistake: nobody would see what she could really do, either. Every muscle coiled, ready to react.

Using his body position, he corralled her out of Lilian's line of sight.

She sidestepped his attempt to touch her ear, and started to—

"You're a shy one, aren't you?" His tone was playful, his grin charming.

What? She gawked at him. That wasn't what an assassin would say. Where was he going with this? "Master Shixian, it wouldn't do to let a man touch me."

"But..." He pointed with that prominent jaw. "You have something in your hair."

She reached up, then scowled. "That's my ear!"

"You...you're an elf!" His mouth formed a perfect circle. "Heavens, forgive me."

"Half-elf." Surely he'd known well before. She searched his eyes.

There was nothing but sincerity. And now, even as close as he was, there was no smell of the sesame ginger, nor any toxin from the Black Lotus' sizeable lexicon. Maybe she'd been mistaken about the Peony Garden's intentions.

"I...I assumed you were half, but I thought you were half-Hua, half-Easterner. Not half-*elf*." He studied her, not like the lechers roving the Floating

World, but with a childlike wonder. It was almost endearing. "I can see it now. There must be quite the story there."

She searched his eyes but found nothing but candid curiosity. The story wouldn't inspire the bards, though—she'd been a bawling babe left at the front gates of the Black Lotus Temple. Master Yan had raised her as his own, though he had lost the only hint of her identity. The letter pinned to her swaddling blanket spoke of a human mother who died giving birth and an elf father too busy to be burdened. Still, she stuck to the same cover story: "I assume I'm like all the few other instances of half-elves. A wanderlust-stricken mother left home, either fell in love or into a trap, and left me with humans."

His expression contorted into genuine concern, unlike any of the other prospective Hummingbirds, who'd just moved on to the next question. He seemed so earnest that it felt cruel to have lied. "Too bad for your mother," he said, "never knowing that her daughter grew into such a beauty."

Nothing but sincerity hung in his tone. Heat rose to the tips of her ears. Of all the handsome young men she'd lusted after, he was even more so. And warm. She would've given herself to him right there and then, if not for the issue of her record Plucking bid. "I am guessing you are not really one of the House guards. Who *are* you, Master Shi—"

"Lieutenant. Lieutenant Chen Shixian. I'm an officer of the Huayuan Provincial Cavalry." He bowed.

Goosebumps prickled on Jie's shoulders, and not from the breeze. While she and horses didn't get along, there was something dashing about a handsome soldier on a horse. "And how did you come to be here? A guest of Lord Peng?"

He shook his head, loosening his luxurious mane, then locked intense eyes on her. "I think you know why I'm here."

Her spine just about turned to jelly. All her pent-up desire felt like a raging torrent about to overrun a dam. If not for the matter of her Plucking bid, she'd take him there and then.

"You have something on your cheek." He reached into the fold of his robe and withdrew a kerchief. It unfurled, revealing intricate stitching, winding in a mesmerizing pattern. The Dragon Weaver magic woven into the cloth washed over her, making her...making her... Heat surged through her. She shook the haze out of her head.

"Are you all right?" Locking those gorgeous eyes on her, he dabbed the kerchief over her cheek. He pulled it back, revealing a dark smudge. He grinned again, so rakish and alluring. "It looks like ash."

Surely she'd cleaned it all off. But that didn't matter. What mattered was that he was now close.

And it didn't bother her.

On the contrary, his body heat and the masculine rust smell sent a jolt up her spine. Fire blossomed inside her.

Their eyes met, searching each other.

"You are so beautiful," he repeated.

Beautiful. Not exotic, or different. Plucking bid be damned. Claiming what little space remained between them, Jie reached up and pulled his face to hers. She parted her lips, and welcomed his tongue.

He pressed against her, boxing her against the wall. His hands slid down her back to her waist, but she moved them lower, up under her skirts. So invited, his fingers brushed along the inside of her thighs, walking higher at a leisurely pace.

Too slow! Aching with heat and desire, she bucked her hips to meet his hand.

He tore her undergarments off. Hooking her right knee into the crook of his elbow, he lifted her leg.

Jie pushed aside his robe to discover his pants down. Finding him erect, she guided it into her.

***

“Sir!” Lilian barked from the archway. “Unhand my Little Sister.”

Jie’s heart lurched. She broke the kiss and looked over Shixian’s shoulder.

At least a dozen people were there. Wide-eyed Blossoms covered their gaping mouths. Men muttered as their lips curled into sneers.

And Lilian. Confusion was scrawled over her face.

The exhilaration from a second before sputtered. Jie pushed herself off Shixian as all heat and drained from her. Her muddled head cleared. Heavens, what had she done?

The Peony Garden Gardener and Lusha pushed through the throng and passed to either side of Lilian. They exchanged knowing smirks.

“You’ve broken the rules of the Floating World, girl.” The Gardener jabbed an accusatory finger at her. “A Blossom may not entertain a Hummingbird in another House without the Gardener’s permission.”

“I thought... I thought...” Brows furrowed, Shixian shook his head. “I wasn’t a Hummingbird.”

Jie nodded. “No. He...he wasn’t. He was...” Oh, Heavens, no.

Holding up Jie's undergarment as if it were a scorpion, Lusha brought her hand to her chest. "Heavens, are you saying you gave in to passion?"

A different kind of heat flared in her cheeks. Was it? What was she thinking? No, there was no thought, just primal desire. For Shixian? He was handsome, for sure, but that alone wasn't enough for her to forget about the value of virginity. No, it had to be...the kerchief. It had Dragon Weaver magic imbued in it. She looked around, but there was no sign of it.

"So much for your Plucking bid." Lusha cast a cruel smile.

This had all been a set-up.

And it'd succeeded.

She'd walked right into it. No matter how much she'd wanted it, even before the magic, she wouldn't have. Not with her Plucking bid at stake. She glared at Shixian.

His eyes widened, and he waved his hand back and forth. "I am so sorry. I didn't know."

"Liar. You used a kerchief embroidered with Artistic Magic."

He shook his head so fast, his head might come off. He was a good actor, that was for sure; maybe not even a military man. "I know nothing about— "

“This?” The Gardener held up a kerchief. No waves of magic rolled off it. “It looks quite plain.”

Had she swapped it? Or was it only single-use? No matter what, there was no proof of what Shixian had done.

The Peony Garden didn’t want her killed, but deflowered. To keep Lusha’s record Plucking bid safe.

And as horrible and underhanded and violating as it was, it left an even more sinister question: who’d tried to kill her this morning, and why?

CHAPTER 9

Though full-fledged Blossoms were allowed to take on lovers as long as it didn't interfere with House business, Florets had no such leeway. Even less so for Jie, whose Plucking bid would've fattened the House's coffers—and the clan's—beyond imagination. In their eyes, it was a dalliance that couldn't go unpunished.

Though technically her contract was held by a Black Lotus shell company, the Gardener had free rein to mete out judgement. She'd stormed over to the Peony Garden, guards in tow. They'd dragged Jie back to the Chrysanthemum Pavillion, and would've confined her to a long-unused cellar if it hadn't stunk like some animal had crawled in there and died. Instead, they locked her in a windowless storehouse, with a guard posted.

With nothing else to do, Jie had just wallowed in what had happened. Even though it'd been a thrilling experience, even though she'd wanted to give herself to Shixian, she wouldn't have.

It was a rape, plain and simple, with embroidered Dragonweaving as the magical means of coercion. With the kerchief, they might be able to prove it and seek redress. Without it, there was no recourse. The Peony Garden would get away with the violation. She'd been tempted to open the high-proof bottles of White Lightning wine stored there to drown her sorrows, or perhaps light the surplus cases of New Year's firecrackers and just end it there and then.

Now, the morning after, as news of her *indiscretion* swirled throughout the Floating World, Jie knelt at the edge of the stage of the Chrysanthemum Pavilion's common room. Arms outstretched, she balanced trays laden with rice wine-filled cups. The entire House gathered below, a witness to her disgrace.

Still, no castigation in the Floating World could begin to compare with everyday Black Lotus training. In the Floating World, no girl, from Sprout to Blossom, was ever whipped, for fear of leaving scars. Kneeling on hardwood planks meant nothing to someone whose body was hardened to stone; and no amount of berating hurt more than Jie's own internal rebuke.

A trap, so obvious, and she'd fallen for it.

And Shixian. For all his charm, he was just manipulating her. Using magic, no less. Her chest clenched. That Turtle's Egg would pay for what he'd taken from her.

Her arms ached, though certainly not as much as anyone else's would in the same position. Definitely not as much as her heart right now.

Gardener Ju hobbled over and jabbed a finger into her chest, daring her to spill any of the rice wine. "I've sent word to the Golden Peacock Company to see what they want to do with you. You'll still fetch an ungodly amount, from all the Hummingbirds who've eyed you over the years."

That was the reality. Lilian's plight made more sense now. All the training as a spy and warrior meant nothing compared to her body's value to wanton men. Jie's heart knotted even more.

"Now, Lord Ting has reserved the entire House for him and Lilian tonight. He wants it empty, so the rest of you have the night off..."

He would've had to pay enough to cover the House's profits for the night. Thousands of *yuan*. It would've been far less expensive to take Lilian to his villa. What kind of depravity did he have in mind?

"...all except Jie. You will serve dinner to Lord Ting and Lilian tonight." The Gardener gestured to the corner of the stage.

Jie looked at the corner, the same one where Lord Ting had lounged two nights before. The same spot she'd cleaned yesterday.

"Maybe he will be your first Hummingbird."

"Gardener!" Lilian dropped to her knees and pressed her forehead to the floor. She looked up. "Little Sister Jie has not yet flowered with Heaven's Dew. She can't receive Hummingbirds yet."

"Gardener!" Speaking in unison, the other girls all dropped to their knees and bowed their heads. Even the Florist, stern but kind mother that she was, joined in.

The Gardener looked among them, lips tight.

Silence fell over the room, save for the soft weeping of Ai and Yin. Jie's heart wound so tight it might burst. Her House sisters, Sprout to Blossom, all supported her, and each other. Just like the Black Lotus Clan members embedded in the Floating World did.

The Gardener's chuff broke the quiet. "Little Jie has lived in the House long enough without earning her keep. Now that the blossom has been plucked, it doesn't matter. Youth is a commodity with diminishing returns, and the fact you've not blossomed with Heaven's Dew makes you even more unique for the Floating World. It will allow us to set an even higher contract price for your regular assignations, and schedule a few a day."

Anger churned in Jie's stomach. The adherence to this one convention had set the Floating World above every other seedy whorehouse in the land. Sure, she was already twenty, but if the Gardener was willing to make this exception now, who would she sacrifice in the future? "Gardener—"

"Silence! Who gave you permission to speak, selfish little slut?" The Gardener's glare shifted from Jie to the Florist. "Send out invitations to all who have bid on her."

The shuddering shoulders and sniffling among the girls intensified. Jie's heart broke more for them than for herself.

"Gardener," Lilian said, pressing her forehead to the ground again. "Please."

The Gardener slammed her hand down on the stage, making everyone wince. "Don't think that just because you are the Chrysanthemum Pavillion's Corsage I won't turn you out. I'll make sure no Floating World House will take you in. Golden Peacock Company will contract you to some back-alley whorehouse in the Trench, where you'll service fifty lowlifes a day."

The Gardener had no idea it was an empty threat, since the Black Lotus Clan would never do such a thing. Lilian knew it, too. She stood, scowling, and took a step forward, in what a trained eye would recognize as the start of an attack.

The room went silent, even as the tension wound tighter than a garrote. The Gardener cowered back, bumping up against the stage as her left leg wobbled.

"I'll do it, willingly," Jie said. Lilian might not have to worry about reprisals from the Gardener, and in fact, banishment from the Floating World was everything she wanted. But the other girls, if emboldened, did not have a clan of spies and assassins to go back to. Jie shot Lilian a warning glance, and would've used signals if her hands weren't full. *The other girls*, she mouthed.

Lilian met her gaze and sighed. Her shoulders slumped and fists unclenched, and she took two steps back and dropped to her knees. "I am sorry, Gardener."

"I'm glad that is settled." The Gardener regained her air of authority, even if her voice came out strained. She turned to Jie and pointed to the corner. "Tonight is an important night. For now, you are going to scrub his favorite table clean and polish every wood surface until I can see your pretty little reflection in them."

* * *

With the cleaning done, along with all her other chores, Jie lay on her side on Lilian's bed, arm supporting her head. Memories of the night before never strayed far from her thoughts. It was times like this that she needed to cuddle in the fluffy white fur of the dogs back at the clan's Black Lotus Monastary.

After repeated rebuffing, Lilian had finally given up trying to comfort her, and now sat at her make-up table in a plain dressing robe, lengthening her lashes. Late afternoon sun streamed in.

Jie finally broke the silence. "What were you thinking, challenging the Gardener?"

"Those are your first words?" Lilian lowered her brush. "I would ask you the same. Don't make this about me. Why did you even go last night? I told you it was dangerous. What if the Peony Garden really wanted to kill you? You never listen."

"I was worried that all our sisters were compromised. I had to hope it was just me."

Lilian's lips pursed. "You should have left it to Wen. She would have figured it out. You always take it upon yourself."

Jie sighed. It was true. Her own hubris, thinking that as senior and with superior senses, nobody could do a better job. But not just that... "I don't want anyone else to get hurt."

"At some point, you have to trust the rest of us."

Jie shook her head. How could she ask others to take risks? "I could never forgive myself if Wen had gotten caught."

"She wouldn't have. She's not as stealthy as you, but she's still good." Lilian glared at her. "Did you ever think that maybe you taking charge of everything has prevented the clan from seeing worth in the rest of us? Maybe that has kept many of us stuck spreading our legs in the Floating World."

Jie's heart sunk. The truths battered her confidence; her very sense of self. Tears threatened.

Lilian rose with enviable grace and glided over. She sat down in the curl formed by Jie's bent knees and body, and draped an arm over her. "Oh, my sweet. I'm so sorry."

Hot tears welled in Jie's eyes and ran down her cheeks.

Lilian climbed over her to the other side of the bed, then embraced Jie from behind. Her cheek pressed against hers. It was protective, comforting.

"I wanted to give myself to him," Jie said. Just saying it made it real. "But I wasn't going to. I couldn't, not with so much money at stake."

Lilian stroked her hair. "I know. Our bodies aren't our own. No matter how much it is drilled into us at the temple, and here in the House, a little piece of me dies every time."

So much sadness in her voice. Jie's stomach twisted. No matter what happened next, she had to convince the clan to reassign Lilian. For now, though, it was time to redirect the conversation. "Clearly, the Peony Garden had ill intentions, but they hadn't planned to go so far as to have me murdered."

"Which means someone else is targeting you." Lilian's nod rubbed against Jie's cheek.

"And maybe not just me."

Lilian's voice dropped lower than a whisper, as if voicing her words too loudly might make them true. "What if there's a traitor? A mole?"

"No." Jie closed her eyes. She'd trained every one of the clan sisters, knew their psychological profiles. "We're like the Steel Orchids. I trust each and every one of them with my life."

"You have a blind spot with us."

Jie started to shake her head, but stopped. She couldn't deny it. Though all clan brothers and sisters felt like family, the girls embedded in the Floating World forged even closer bonds. If one wanted to betray them, the rest wouldn't see it coming. "You're right. We need to contact the clan, to implement an objective evaluation."

"When?"

"Now." Jie started to rise.

Lilian held her down. "I'll go. There's still time before Lord Ting arrives."

"Masked Crossbowman saw you, too. It's too dangerous."

"Trust me. Trust my skill." The message was the same as just a few minutes earlier. Cupping Jie's cheeks, Lilian leaned in with a deep kiss.

Every nerve tingled, up and down her spine, to her toes and fingertips. Jie reached around to the small of Lilian's back and the nape of her neck, drawing her closer.

Lilian broke the kiss, and smiled. "I'll be all right."

Jie gave a tentative nod.

Stripping off her dressing robe, revealing her glorious figure, Lilian went to her secret floor compartment.

"I wore your stealth suit yesterday, and got it dirty going up the chimney. It's under Little Wen's bed in the Peony Garden."

"So that's how you got out." Lilian giggled, shaking her head. She went to her wardrobe and withdrew a dark shirt and pair of pants, and put them on. She twirled as if showing off a new dress. "How do I look?"

Stunning, even in plain clothes. A grin tugged at Jie's lips, unbidden. "Like a pig."

With a pig-like snort, Lilian opened her window shutters and climbed out.

A bad feeling twisted Jie's gut; the feeling that maybe that kiss would be her last memory of Lilian.

CHAPTER 10

Waiting in Lilian's dressing area, Jie applied make-up appropriate for a full-fledged Blossom, for what might her first assignation. With Lilian gone, Jie had cried until her tears ran dry, and now had dark rings under her eyes. Not even the powder foundation could hide them, so she applied paste concealer and kohl eyeliner. It was amazing she could keep a steady hand while worry tied her stomach in knots.

Dusk cast long shadows over the Floating World, and Lilian had yet to return.

All the girls had already left. From the sound of it, the kitchen staff had finished preparations and were getting ready to leave as well. Logs in the common room hearth crackled, the sound and heat carrying through the flues and into Lilian's room.

Hidden among the other noises were the sounds of hands and feet climbing up the wall.

Jie let out a sigh of relief and ran to the window, throwing open the shutters.

Little Wen's eyes widened. "Elder Sister! How did you hear me? Of course you heard me."

All her worries rushed back, cutting short her joy at seeing Wen. Jie helped her climb in. "What are you doing here?"

Wen brushed off her stealth suit, which embellished her curves even more than her gowns. "Lilian came to me. When I told her I'd found out where Masked Crossbowman ate, she decided to use herself as bait. She wants you to go there as backup."

Blood drained from Jie's head. Lilian wouldn't stand a chance. "Meet me outside the kitchen door."

Wen climbed back through the window; snatching up a high-collared, dark-blue gown, Jie rushed out to the balcony overlooking the common room. The Gardener and Florist were talking in Lord Ting's favorite corner, setting a feast at the round table and making a last check to make sure everything was perfect before they left for the night.

Zigzagging over the safe spots of the nightingale floors, Jie dashed to the stairwell, descended, and reached the room she shared with the Florets and Seedlings. She retrieved a dagger and throwing stars from her chest's false bottom, and put on her stealth suit. She threw the dark-blue outer gown on over it.

Only a few minutes had passed by the time she returned to the hallway to the common room.

The Gardener and Florist were blocking the way to the kitchens, so she stayed low and crept over to the main door. Opening it just wide enough, she slipped out.

The vantage point gave her a good view of the main gates, where Lord Ting and his entourage of four men waited, their crimson livery ablaze even in the low light. He stood taller and broader than the rest, a man among boys. They were surrendering their swords and daggers to the gate guards, per the customs and conventions of the Floating World. For their part, the guards took longer than usual, no doubt instructed by the Gardener to stall until Lilian came down from her room—not knowing that Lilian was missing.

"You can keep that," the guard said, motioning to what looked like a wooden club, which one of Lord Ting's men presented.

The other's sash moved stiffly when he withdrew his scabbarded sword, as if a launderer had used too much starch. Jie stared at it for a moment, but Lilian's safety took priority. She tore her gaze away and ran along the side of the mansion to the rear, through the kitchen's side door and out the back.

Wen waited there, her expression scrunched up. She beckoned. "Come on. It's a stand outside Yue Heaven."

"No, you go light the lantern at the Black Lotus Shrine, then go to the safehouse." With a shake of her head, Jie took off down the alleys toward the Yue Heaven.

With the Floating World coming to life, she paused at intersections with major streets, and used the shadows cast by the red lanterns to move unseen and unheard. Laughing men filtered in for a night of adventure and debauchery, providing plenty of cover.

The scent of sesame-ginger grew stronger until she froze at the side of an opium den. Across the street stood the recently-opened Yue Heaven. Boasting euphoric properties, it came from a tree in the North, and the Imperial Court promoted it as a cheaper alternative to opium. Its only side-effects were increased libido and food cravings, which was probably why there was a stand beside it selling pork and vegetables on a skewer. The vendor, head wrapped in a kerchief, grilled the food behind a makeshift bar with six stools. Two men in guards' robes sat together, chatting. There was no sign of Lilian.

Maybe Masked Crossbowman and his comrades had already captured her, and Jie had arrived too late to help.

Heart racing, Jie checked both directions, gauging the way the crowds turned their heads. With the blind spots timed, she kept low and darted across the street, until she stood behind the vendor. The aroma of sesame and ginger drowned out all other smells.

Modulating her voice to a deeper timbre, she threw it with the clan's *Ghost Echo* technique to make it sound like it was coming from the two men. "That Ju Lilian of the Chrysanthemum Pavilion is a beauty!"

"She sure is," the vendor said, nodding as he turned over skewers, but thankfully not looking up.

"Wasn't she here earlier?" Jie asked.

"Haven't seen her recently." The vendor shook his head.

Jie sucked on her lower lip. Lilian had never even made it here. Maybe the conspirators had captured her.

"Huh?" One of the men turned away from his companion to look at the vendor.

"Didn't you ask about Ju Lilian?"

"Who's that?"

"The Corsage of the Chrysanthemum Pavilion," the vendor said. "Didn't you just mention her?"

The men exchanged glances, and with a coordinated snort, got up and left.

Something didn't add up, but there was still one shot in the dark. Or four shots in a shaded alley. Looking left and right to gauge interest in the stand, she went around to the front. "Excuse me."

The vendor looked up. "What would you like to order?"

Jie bowed, shaking her head when she straightened. "I'm looking for a Hummingbird."

His eyes roved over her. "Aren't you the Chrysanthemum Pavilion's half-elf?"

"Yes." She covered her mouth with a hand, an admittedly clunky gesture compared to other Blossoms. "I was supposed to meet a man with a Repeater here."

His brow furrowed. "A crossbow?"

She nodded.

"I have a regular who sometimes carries a crossbow around. He was here earlier with three, four friends. In fact, they were taking a repeating crossbow apart."

A standard military Repeater. Craftsmen specialized in making the individual components, while trained assemblers mass-produced them. Why would—Jie's blood ran colder than ice. "What were they wearing?"

"Crimson robes. Looked to be guards for a noble house."

"Did one have a scar?" Jie ran a finger across her forehead.

"Is that your Humm—"

Jie turned and raced back toward the Chrysanthemum Pavilion. It all made sense now. In the Peony Garden last night, the Artist wasn't framing a picture of desperate men, he was lining up a target. With the two Houses being near-exact replicas, that target could be no other than Lord Ting, who would be sitting in his favorite corner right now. His own men had smuggled the Repeater parts past the House guards, where one would reassemble it inside. But why?

She skidded to a halt as the House guards stopped her at the gates, holding a light up to her face.

"Little Jie," one said. "The Gardener is looking all over for you. How did you get out?"

Pushing past them, she shed the gown as she bolted across the courtyard. She threw open the doors and ran into the common room.

Lord Ting sat in his favorite corner, sipping from a cup, a frown plastered to his face. "They said she had a surprise for me, but I've been waiting for an hour. Where is she?"

Standing at his side with a decanter of rice wine in hand, the Florist bowed low. "My apologies, my Lord."

Up and to the left, the head of a repeating crossbow peeked out from the shadows of the mezzanine.

"Get down!" Jie yelled, sprinting between tables and chairs.

Lord Ting turned to her, eyes wide. The Florist gawked, but stood transfixed. Four of his men flashed crimson in her peripheral vision, converging on her. One had a large scar on his forehead.

The crossbow clicked in rapid succession.

To Jie's eye, the two bolts flew in slow motion toward Lord Ting and the Florist, yet she ran even slower. She could only save one. A kind but stern mother figure? Or a loyal lord, who was instrumental to maintaining peace in the unsettled North?

A few feet away, one of his men reached out to grab Jie, but she turned to the side, just avoiding him. She leaped with an outstretched hand...

...and swiped the bolt out of the air.

The Florist's screams ceased, replaced by a gurgle.

Jie sprawled across the table, sliding face-first over and though succulent food, smashing porcelain dishes. With a slap of her hands, she popped herself into a flip and landed in a crouch between Lord Ting and the crossbowman. Any second now, more bolts would fly.

None came.

Jie's eyes blurred, and her balance swayed. A heady scent attacked her nose—deer musk, a key component of a clan contact toxin used on females—clung to the crossbow bolt in her hand. Meaning Lilian had been right about a traitor and Jie's blind spot. Whoever it was had even surmised Jie would catch the bolt.

But who? The Florist's ragged, dying breaths made it impossible to concentrate. Through the darkness encroaching on her vision, Jie squinted toward the balcony. A female form appeared at the edge of the shadows with the crossbow.

Little Wen? It was hard to see, but it made logical sense. She must've helped capture Lilian, then drawn Jie away so they could assassinate Lord Ting.

The crossbow clicked again, the sound echoing behind her. A bolt flew.

Jie swept a hand out.

It zipped past her.

Lord Ting grunted and slumped forward

Jie collapsed back onto the table as all went black.

CHAPTER 11

The scent of ammonia assaulted Jie's senses, jolting her awake. Her head felt as if a dwarf had forged an axe on it. She was sitting in a chair, hands behind her back on either side of the chair's spindle. She went to stand, but rope bit into her wrists. Cord bound her feet together. She blinked several times to clear her vision, and the blurriness crystalized into focus.

Lord Ting sat slumped over in a chair by her side, with a crossbow bolt protruding from his back and a line of blood drying on the side of his mouth. Florist Wei, too, sat dead in another chair, head lolled to the left, unseeing gaze seemingly locked on Jie. One of Lord Ting's traitorous guards leered at her, eyes hungry, but then joined the others in walking to and from the kitchens, carrying crates of clinking bottles and setting them near the hearth. Another stacked bedding and linens near the main entrance. The scent of sesame-ginger mingled in with the coppery tang of blood.

Little Wen had made a mistake: she'd left Jie alive, with her feet bound but not immobilized. Once she escaped, she'd bring the wrath of the clan down on her. "Wen! What did you do with Lilian?"

A melodious laugh broke out behind her. "Nothing."

Jie's blood ran cold as she twisted to look over her shoulder. No, it couldn't be.

"Not Little Wen. She worships the ground you walk on." Lilian sashayed around to the front. Her loose, baggy pants allowed her to easily straddle Jie. Sighing, she cupped her cheek. "I told you you had a blind spot."

No, no, no. Tears flew as Jie shook her head. "Why? Why did you do this?"

"I told you," Lilian said. "I wanted out of this life. I'd held out hope that you'd be able to convince Master Yan to reassign me, but here's the truth: I played the Little Sister you adored for too long, and the clan thinks—thought— all I'm good for is sating Lord Ting's desires."

Jie's fault. All Jie's fault. "I can convince Master Yan. I swear."

Lilian shook her head. "This was my last chance to get out."

"The clan will hunt you down," Jie said, not with malice, but with an affection she couldn't deny, despite the betrayal.

"Not if they think I am dead." She gestured to a body near the hearth.

The man who'd posed as a drunkard. Jie gasped. "You stored him in that cellar. That's where the stench came from. You used a ruse, thinking I would kill him when he attacked."

"No. You were always a threat to the plan, and I'd originally planned on removing you altogether." With a sigh, she looked up at one of the men, whose gait marked him as Masked Crossbowman. "I couldn't bring myself to do it, and trusted your blind spot."

"She already killed one of your comrades," Jie yelled to Masked Crossbowman, hoping to drive a wedge between them. "What's to keep her from sacrificing you next?"

Masked Crossbowman paused, the bottles in his crate clinking. "Lin ran his mouth too much. We were going to kill him anyway. Less ways to split the reward."

Reward. Someone had ordered the hit on Lord Ting, enough for his men to turn on him. Jie turned back to Lilian. "How did you even get the body here?"

Lilian gestured toward the other men. "With help, of course, while you were warning the other girls."

"You never went to the safehouse to warn the clan."

"No. I needed the clan *not* to get further involved."

So all the failings were Jie's. She'd trusted Lilian implicitly. Now, she looked at the crates the men were stacking near the hearth. "The White Lightning and firecrackers. You are going to set the House on fire."

"Inspired by the training accident twenty years ago." There was no satisfaction in Lilian's voice, only sorrow. "I made sure all the girls and staff would be gone, and the distance from the mansion to the courtyard will keep the flames from spreading to the rest of the Floating World. The Gardener even agreed to douse the compound walls because I said they were too dirty for Lord Ting's visit."

She'd tried to minimize collateral damage; Lilian wasn't totally ruthless. Maybe there was still hope to turn her away from this path. Jie tilted her head toward the Florist. "What about her?"

Lilian shook her head. "An unfortunate casualty, but her body is more likely to be mistaken for mine than the other one."

Jie clenched her teeth. Anger welled inside her.

"I was worried you might figure it all out when the Gardener confined you to that specific storehouse."

"I was too busy crying over what that man did to me. Did you plan that, too?"

"No!" Lilian's eyes widened. "Of course not. I never wanted you going to the Peony Garden at all, because then you'd find out they had nothing to do with Masked Crossbowman. I even told the Gardener to keep a guard at the door and below the window, and used a dwarf lock, which you somehow picked."

The lock which hadn't been there when Lilian had left the House hours ago. Jie had overlooked it then, even though it was glaringly obvious now.

"I never imagined they would do that to you. Before I leave the Floating World forever, I will poison the Peony Garden's Gardener, ruin Lusha's face, and castrate your rapist."

Jie's chest swelled at the ferociousness in Lilian's voice. Conflicting emotions tore at her. Here was someone who loved her, but had also considered killing her. Who'd tried to arrange a hit on her, but then backed out. She shook her head. "Your plan was worthy of the Architect, except that you left me alive."

Lilian brushed her cheek, the softness of her curves and her honeysuckle scent intoxicating. She leaned in and whispered in her ear. "Don't you see? I never even wanted you here. When I left earlier, it was to trick Wen into getting you as far away as possible."

"So I wouldn't foil your assassination?"

"So I wouldn't have to make you choose between me and the clan."

"But you knew I'd come back. The crossbow bolt was meant for me to catch."

Lilian nodded. "A good plan always takes into account unlikely factors. Like this one. Join me. We can start our own clan. A sisterhood. The ones who contracted me to kill Lord Ting will pay well for our skills. Please."

"I can't just betray the clan that adopted me."

"You have thirty seconds to decide." Lilian squeezed tight. "Please."

"Are you sure this is what you want to do? No one will ever have to know you were involved in this plot."

Lilian shook her head violently. "Then I'll just be spreading my legs at some other House."

"I understand." Jie brought her heels up to the edge of the seat, sliding Lilian closer into her lap. Jie leaned into her.

The tension in Lilian's shoulders relaxed, and her smile looked so genuinely relieved.

Jie kicked back against the table. The force sent the chair tipping back. She thrust her legs to increase her speed, and yanked on her wrists as they crashed. The chair splintered under their weight, and Jie's hands, while still bound, broke free from the remnants of the chair. She continued her backward roll, ending up on her tied feet, between Lilian's shins where she lay prone.

Turning onto her side, Lilian scissored her legs at the front of Jie's ankles and the back of her knees, but Jie leapt, drawing her knees to her chest and swinging her bound arms under her and to the front. Her feet hit the ground just as Lilian windmilled her legs up and flipped over into a crouch, one fist to the ground.

Lord Ting's men all paused mid-stride, gawking.

"You tricked me!" Lilian sprung up and surged forward with a barrage of punches.

Jie hopped back onto the table and snatched up a pottery shard. Spinning away from the attacks, she sawed through the bindings on her feet. She slid off, putting the table between them.

Lord Ting's men now set down the crates and stormed over with knives and cleavers from the kitchen. Two came around either side of the table, while Lilian leaped onto it with a dagger drawn.

Jie flipped the table up onto its side, throwing Lilian back, just as both men fell on her. One chopped down with a cleaver, but Jie lifted her bound wrists into its path. The blade nicked her forearm, but frayed the rope enough for her to pull her hands free.

Now entirely mobile, she spun out of the line of the other's stab. In the same motion, she pushed the table, sending its far legs slamming into the first man. He stumbled into the second, and Jie seized his wrist, twisted the knife around, and let him impale himself on the point. His eyes bulged, and she plucked his weapon away.

The survivor stared, dumbfounded at the turn of events. He lunged at her, but she slipped past him in the direction he'd come and pushed the table so that the leg clotheslined him. She yanked the crossbow bolt from Lord Ting's back and stabbed the man through his eye.

A musky scent stuck to her hand. Stupid half-elf! The toxin! With only a few more seconds of consciousness, she pulled the table down.

Lilian was gone, and given the way Jie'd spun the table right and left, blocking her view, Lilian could've used any of the exits, save for the kitchen.

The two surviving men, Scar Head and Masked Crossbowman—now unmasked—were running toward the main entrance. Torches in hand, they lit banners, paintings, and anything flammable along the way. Fire already raged in the two archways between the common room and the kitchens and conservatory. Meanwhile, a line of firepowder crackled and sizzled in a flash of light. It would ignite the improvised explosive before Jie could reach the makeshift fuse.

Thank the Heavens: the active ingredient of the toxin must've evaporated. Tucking the bolt away, she started toward the main entrance.

The men set the pile of bedding ablaze, blocking that route of escape.

With only seconds to escape the initial blast, she bolted to the hall, toward the veranda. She yanked on each set of double doors, only to find them barred from the outside.

An explosion erupted from the common room hearth. Timbers cracked and glass shattered. Firecrackers burst in a staccato beat. A fireball billowed toward her. She turned the corner and raced to the bathhouse. Crashing through the doors of the first room, she dove into the tub. Flames shot above her, filling the room with reds and oranges before receding.

Jie surfaced, but avoided taking a breath of the hot, choking air. The towels and robes were all burning, filling the room with smoke. She climbed out of the tub and, staying low, crawled to the hallway.

The moist wood hadn't caught, but it wouldn't be long before the fire from the rest of the mansion reached here. The servants' door had been blasted open. Jie scuttled through the hall and leaped through the exit.

She gulped in the cooler fresh air, and looked.

Flames raged from every window of the Chrysanthemum Pavilion's main mansion. Wood crackled, and ash floated on the smoke. From outside the compound walls, bells clanged and people shouted.

Finding out which way Lilian had escaped would take time, especially since the orange glow from the flames kept Jie's elf vision from kicking in and assessing the area around the mansion. The two surviving accomplices, however...

CHAPTER 12

First patting soot onto her face, Jie dashed around to the front of the burning mansion. The gate guards approached, running halfway between the main gate and the mansion.

Jie sprinted to meet them. "What happened to Lord Ting's men?"

Giving her a look from head to toe and back, the first guard pointed to the main gate. "They left to bring help."

Unlikely. "Did they claim their weapons?"

The guard nodded.

Bidding them farewell, Jie dashed out the front door to search. They couldn't be more than a few minutes ahead, though they had the advantage of knowing where they were going.

She sniffed. Hidden among the soot and ash smell, and the gathering crowds, was the sesame-ginger marinade. Using her nose, she followed the ever-stronger scent.

The neighborhood fire brigade ran by, laden with buckets, bamboo ladders, and poles, the colors of their blue uniforms flashing.

They passed, revealing the two men striding across the bridge out of the Floating World. One carried a Repeater, which the House guard had failed to mention.

Jie stuck to the shadows as she pursued them into the abandoned silk market. Inside, with the tent blotting out the moons and stars, her elf vision transformed the shadowed, empty stands into hues of green and grey. Though human eyes supposedly couldn't see as well in the dark, she still stayed low as she trailed them.

They paused at several stalls, looking back toward the entrance, and wagged their fingers. They were counting, trying to locate a specific stand.

"This is the one," one said.

"Are you sure? I'm counting three down, two over."

"That's what she said." The other threw his hands up.

"Just drop it off, then."

One knelt and stashed something under the table.

Jie sucked on her lower lip. Whatever else Lilian was, she was right about Jie's cavalier approach. She should've recruited clan sisters to help, because no matter her skills, she couldn't be in three places at once. Now, she had to choose: follow these men; wait for them to leave to see what they'd left behind, and who came to retrieve it; or track down Lilian.

"All right. Good job tonight. I'll see you tomorrow." One of the men saluted the other with a palm in his fist, head bowed.

The other returned the gesture.

If only there were four of her! She dashed up to them as they turned from each other, and pulled Masked Crossbowman's dagger from his sash. Reaching up and covering his mouth with a hand, she slashed his throat. She caught his crossbow before it clattered to the ground, then eased his body down.

She turned to chase after Scar Head. Just before he reached the edge of the tent, she caught up. She extended an arm—

He spun around, his broadsword sweeping from its scabbard.

Jie rolled backward under the weapon's arc, then backhand-sprung over his follow-up. She landed on one of the tables in a defensive crouch.

"You!" he said. "You just won't die."

"I'm like a cockroach." And in the dark, she had an advantage. Jie threw her voice to the side with *Ghost Echo*.

He chopped down toward the perceived source, his broadsword lodging into the table and sending a reverberation into Jie's feet. He yanked on the weapon to free it.

Jie darted over and slashed his palmar tendons.

He screamed as his fingers went slack about the hilt, but also whipped a dagger out with his other hand and stabbed.

She jumped to the other side of the table, then crawled under it. She threw her voice behind him. "Over here!"

When he turned his back to her, she severed his Achilles tendons. He buckled to his knees, but kept slashing back and forth with his dagger.

Jie came out behind him and cut through his triceps, locking his elbow in a bent position and rendering his weapon useless. She pulled his hair back, bringing him to the ground.

"Now," she said, stabbing the tip of her dagger into his cheek. "You will die tonight. Answer my questions, and it will be quick. Who hired you?"

"Your whore sister," he said through gritted teeth.

Jie dug deeper, eliciting a scream.

"I swear it. Our Lord has been her patron for a year—"

"*Had* been. You betrayed him. Now, go on."

"And she'd talk to us, all sweet." He sniffled. "She slept with us."

"Impossible. She'd never sleep with her patrons' guards, and you couldn't afford her."

"She loved us. It was true, genuine affection."

As any other Night Blossom except Jie could fake. She snorted. Lilian had set these men up.

"Well...." His face scrunched up, and he opened his mouth to speak, but then shut it.

Jie knew why. Her blind spot was obvious even to him. "Say it. I promise I won't hurt you more for the answer."

His eyes flitted to the blade. "Maybe you don't know her as well as you think."

Clearly not. "I've never seen you or the other three at the House."

He shook his head. "Only his most trusted guards went with him to the Floating World."

"And yet, he got stuck with a pack of traitors today, of all days."

"She had us poison their food. They were all sick today."

So Lilian had set herself up as the planner, fixer, recruiter, and operative. The clan had drastically underestimated her. Jie had drastically underestimated her. The blind spot. "So, you kill your lord, what then?"

"She said there'd be a reward and a new job, but never said where."

Jie looked over to the table where they'd dropped the package. "What did you leave under that table?"

"A message."

"Who is picking it up?"

"I don't know. She just told us to leave it there."

Jie sucked on her lower lip. If Lilian had wanted the message for herself, she would have gotten it from them at the Peony Garden. As was, she likely didn't want to be seen making contact with whoever planned to retrieve it.

Meanwhile, Masked Crossbowman seemed to be fading in and out of consciousness. In the bigger picture, he was just a pawn, and there was no point in making him suffer. His was a necessary death, lest rumors of real Black Fists get out. "As promised," she said, "I will make your death quick."

After slashing his throat, she went over to the table and retrieved the message. No seal, just a honeysuckle scent and Jie's own name written on it.

With trembling fingers, Jie unfolded the message and looked. It was a poem recounting the parting of lovers, written in Lilian's graceful hand. But she'd embellished certain words in a way that only a Black Lotus clan member would be able to decipher:

My Sweet. I am happy you found this, because it means that you survived. However, you also fell into my last trap. While you followed Ping's men, my trail has gotten colder. You were always too impulsive. Goodbye, my sweet. I've always loved you.

Jie's gut wrenched, twisted by conflicting emotions. She started to crumple the message up, but then stopped. This might be her last memento of Lilian. No matter how events had unfolded, she'd tried to keep Jie out of danger; and when that failed, attempted to turn her away from the clan. Even now, she would exact vengeance on the Peony Garden and—

Jie sucked in a breath. There was one last chance to track Lilian down.

CHAPTER 13

With the crowds gathering outside the conflagration of the Chrysanthemum Pavilion, the streets were nearly empty. Jie still kept to the back alleys, to avoid questions about why a half-elf in a stealth suit was running around. She paused only when she spotted a clan sister on her way to the shrine, and signed, *Come to the Peony Garden.*

Despite Jie's scandal the previous night, red banners hung from the Peony Garden's gates, in honor of Young Lord Peng Kai-Zhi's imminent First Pollinating. Two House guards stood at the main gate, but beyond, there was none of the usual chatter or sound of musical instruments coming from the mansion. Jie had seen the Peony Garden girls among the crowds outside the Chrysanthemum Pavilion.

She crept around to the back, and like the night before, entered through the empty kitchens. Even the hearth stood cold. Jie went over to it and listened, in case any whispers echoed through the shared flue system.

"I didn't know," moaned a disembodied male voice. Shixian's voice.

Jie's gut clenched, not with the pleasant butterflies from the night before, but with anger. He was upstairs, either in the Gardener's room or Lusha's.

"The Gardener told me she'd paid for it," he said. "That it was a gift. I didn't know about the virgin price. I swear. I—"

His scream cut short his words. A female shriek joined his.

Jie darted to the empty common room, leaped up to a tabletop, then pop-vaulted off a column to grab the floor of the mezzanine in front of the Gardener's room. She pulled herself up, flipped over the railing, and went to the door. No sound came from within, but Jie slid the door open and peeked inside.

The Gardener lay sprawled on the bed, sightless eyes open, blood flecking her lips. A cup rested on a table, but no steam wafted above it. Jie padded in and sniffed. Yue bark toxin, near imperceptible to a human's frail nose, and fatal in just a few minutes. The poor woman must've sipped the tea, started to feel light-headed, and then gone to lay down, never to wake up.

The Gardener deserved many things for what she'd done to Jie, but death?

Another scream echoed in the hearth, this time closer.

Jie ran out, climbed to the top of the mezzanine rail, and then jumped to catch the floor of the third-floor balcony. She pulled herself up, flipped over, and tried the door.

Locked.

Jie went through the next door, into another Blossom's room. She climbed through the window, shimmied over to Lusha's, and looked in.

In the area lit by a bauble lamp, ropes bound Shixian spread-eagled to the posts of Lusha's bed. Sweat beaded on his pale face, and he whimpered as he looked toward a bloodstain on his crotch. On the other side of the bed, cord suspended Lusha's tied hands to the rafters. Lines of blood trickled from multiple wounds on her face. A bloody cloth served as a gag.

Lilian had meted out all the vengeance Jie had sworn, when she'd knelt all alone in the storeroom the night before. From the sound of Lilian's soft sniffling to the side, she hadn't found it easy. Despite all she'd done, she was still sweet, gentle Lilian.

Jie's heart ached more at what she had to do now. She took a deep breath and bounded through the window, rolling over the carpet. A throwing star whirled at her head, and she handsprung out of its way. Twisting midair, she landed in a crouch, fist to the ground, dagger in her other hand.

Five paces away, Lilian presented her side, a noble's curved *dao* sword lifted over her shoulder with both hands. "How—?"

"Don't you remember? You told me you'd come here to punish them."

Lilian let out a cute laugh; the way her lips quirked stirred fond memories. "I guess you're not the only one with a blind spot."

"No." But maybe it had been meant to lull Jie into a mistake. She looked around for potential traps. "You planned everything so well, I'm surprised you didn't predict the possibility of a final confrontation."

"Who says I didn't?" Lilian raised an eyebrow.

"Because I suspect I would already be dead." Jie gauged possible lines of attack. Before tonight, she would never have considered the sword's longer reach to be an advantage, not in Lilian's hands. Now, though... She feinted with a stab.

The blade flashed into the space where she would've been, faster than Lilian had ever wielded it.

"You are full of surprises," Jie said.

Lilian snapped back into a ready stance. "I've always held back. Just like you taught me."

"You always let the other sisters win, then." Jie stayed at the edge of the sword's reach, ready to attack again. "To hide your true ability."

No, that wasn't it, judging by the way Lilian's lips pursed for a split second. She'd done it because she was a good person. She lowered her weapon. "I'm not going back."

"The clan wouldn't take you back, after what you've done. I have no choice but to bring you in for questioning."

"Or let me go."

"You know I can't do that." Jie lunged again, avoiding the chop, and stabbed.

Lilian slipped out of the first attack, then the follow-up, and riposted with an upward slash.

Jie dodged, but pain seared in her side. She looked down to see a split in the stealth suit, and the fine line of blood from a shallow wound. With a shorter blade and apparently equal skill, she was at a disadvantage. Jie jumped back and plucked the light bauble from the lamp.

She dropped it to the floor and crushed it underfoot. Her elf vision kicked in as the light winked out. She threw a grunt to Lilian's side with a *Ghost Echo*.

Turning her back on Jie, Lilian swept her sword through the spot.

Jie surged forward, seizing Lilian's wrist. She leaped up feet-first and wrapped them around Lilian's arm. The sword slipped out of her grasp, and its tip lodged into the floor. Jie leaned back to hyperextend Lilian's elbow, but she bent it, grabbing her wrist with the other hand. She thrust her shoulder down, slamming Jie into the hardwood floors.

The shock knocked the air from Jie's lungs, and her fingers went limp on Lilian's arm.

Lilian pulled her arm free, stood, and ran to the door. When she opened it, light from the common room flooded in.

Wheezing, Jie popped back onto her feet and staggered into pursuit.

Lilian threw herself over the mezzanine and dropped down so her feet landed on the railing below. She ran along it to the next column and slid down to the first floor. With a last look at Jie, she ran through the front door.

Jie gave chase, following the same route down to the first floor.

Lilian came back through the doors, then closed and barred them. She spun to face Jie, knife in hand. Her eyes spoke of fear.

"What is it?" Jie pointed her dagger at the doors.

"The clan sisters."

Jie closed her eyes and listened. Though their feet padded lightly, she could hear the daughters of the Black Lotus fanning out around the mansion. She opened her eyes. "They are spreading out to block every route of escape. You can't beat us all. Just tell me who hired you to kill Lord Ting, so the clan won't torture it out of you."

Lilian walked over, shaking her head. "Oh, Jie. I don't know. Whoever it was knew that Lord Ting was my patron, and left a message offering me enough money to buy out my contract. I went to the meeting place, only to find another message with a vial and instructions to poison Ting. It was a crude mixture, one which he would've noticed before he drank enough to kill him. I left a message saying as much, and told my new employer to leave it to me. We've been corresponding ever since."

"And you did all this? Not knowing who your employer was?" Jie looked around, gauging how close the other sisters were. They'd reach the common room in moments. "It could've been the clan, testing you!"

Lilian shrugged. "I decided months ago that I was through with the clan, one way or the other."

"Where are you exchanging messages?"

"I drop my messages off under the lucky cat figurine at the Jade Teahouse, and pick up messages from the same grove of trees the clan uses."

These clues might help in uncovering Lilian's employer, though no doubt he'd go to ground.

Black Lotus Sisters appeared on the mezzanine and archways in perfect synchronization. Jie would have felt pride if it weren't for the heaviness in her heart.

"What's happening?" Wen asked, expression contorted into confusion.

Yuna started to climb over the handrail.

Holding up a hand, Jie signaled them to hold back.

Lilian looked up at them and gave a wry smile. "Let this be our last dance."

Tears threatened to blur Jie's vision, but she blinked them away. "There has to be another way. The Viper's Rest, maybe." The dangerous technique would make someone appear dead, though it ran the risk of making them forget who they were.

Shaking her head, Lilian lunged with her knife. Their blades flashed as Jie backed up, ceding ground. It couldn't end. Not this way. There had to be some way to disarm and capture Lilian, and convince the clan to give her a second chance. Though practical, Master Yan wasn't coldhearted. Surely he'd understand the toll the Floating World took on the girls.

"Come on!" Lilian slashed in a zigzag, with deadly precision. No matter the affection between them, she gave no quarter. Around them, the girls all murmured.

"Jie!" Little Wen threw a shortsword over.

Lilian caught the scabbard, but Jie seized the hilt. She pulled the weapon free. With a blade in either hand, Jie renewed her half-hearted attacks.

"Dead." Lilian jabbed her in the chest with the scabbard, then bludgeoned her side with the backstroke. "Dead. Come on, honor me with a good fight. I'm not going to hold back anymore." Her eyes glinted with a deadly focus. She unleashed an onslaught of stabs with the knife and swings with the scabbard like never before, this time with intent to kill.

Jie's automatic reflexes kicked in. Slipping through the barrage, she cut Lilian's forearm, sending the knife clattering from her limp fingers, then sliced through the scabbard. The other end spun back, slashing Lilian across the cheek.

Blood flowed from the open wounds. Lilian staggered into Jie, knocking her down. The weight bore down on her.

Lilian lifted herself up. Her tear-filled eyes met Jie's before sweeping over the room. "They're all watching."

"It doesn't matter." Jie shook her head. If only she'd realized before she'd come to the Peony Garden. "These aren't fatal wounds." She started to throw the knife away.

Lilian caught her wrist. Blood flecked her lips. Her eyes searched Jie's. "Set me free."

Master Yan wasn't coldhearted, but he was practical. The clan could never truly set Lilian free, not after this betrayal. Tears blurred Jie's vision. If only she'd let her go before. Now, there really was no choice. She thrust the knife into Lilian's neck.

The light went out of her eyes, and her body slumped. Jie scuttled up to her knees and rested Lilian's head in her lap.

Jie had done this. If her chest squeezed any harder, her heart would burst. She fought to take in a breath.

Around them, some clan sisters sniffled, while others openly sobbed.

Gaze dropping to her lap, Jie brushed matted hair out of Lilian's face. Her expression looked so...peaceful. If only things had turned out differently. Any number of decisions would have led to a different outcome. She could've broken off pursuit after killing the last two men. Or even before that, not returned to the Chrysanthemum Pavillion in a futile attempt to save Lord Ting.

Or even over the years, when her own blind spot had kept her from recognizing Lilian's skills, maybe trapping her in the Floating World.

One of Jie's tears plopped onto Lilian's cheek. She could have killed Jie on multiple occasions tonight, but had held back. In the end, it had been her decision to return here to punish the members of the Peony Garden, and her choice to sacrifice herself for Jie.

Wiping the tears from her eyes, Jie took a deep breath and cleared her throat. She straightened and fought to keep her voice steady. "Lilian was a traitor and deserved her fate."

They each sank to a knee, fist to the ground, head bowed. "Yes, Eldest Sister."

Jie nodded. "Little Wen, go to the safehouse and bring a Cleaner. The rest of you, start removing evidence. The Gardener is dead in her room, and the Corsage and her Hummingbird are witnesses on the third floor."

And there was still the matter of who'd turned Lilian. Jie would hunt him down and exact vengeance.

EPILOGUE

In the Peony Garden, the expert work of the Black Lotus Cleaners left no evidence of Lilian's rampage. Bound and drugged, Lusha and Shixian had been taken, along with the Gardener's body, to a Triad-infested neighborhood outside the city walls. Salacious rumors about unpaid debts circulated throughout the Floating World.

The fire at the Chrysanthemum Garden had been spun as an unfortunate kitchen accident. With it being a burnt-out husk of its former glory, its Blossoms, Seedlings, and Florets all found new homes at the other great Houses of the Floating World.

All except Jie. After burying Lilian at the Black Lotus Temple's cemetery for adepts, she returned to the safehouse just outside of the Floating World. Evidence from that fateful night lay on the floor of one of the rooms: the murder weapon, crossbow bolts, ledgers and records from the Peony Garden, and everything recovered from the Chrysanthemum Pavilion. She spent sleepless days and nights poring through it all, and retracing the steps of Lilian's accomplices.

That was how her adopted father, Master Yan, found her a week after that fateful night. Though he usually managed to evade even her keen senses, he'd brought someone with him. A child, from the sound of the footsteps. Maybe some new girl, about to enter the Floating World as a Seedling.

The door opened, and she turned.

Even at middle age, Master Yan did not look young or old. His face was so plain, he could mingle into almost any crowd and never be remembered. So unlike her, the half-elf with exotic features.

"Greetings, my daughter."

She bowed her head. "Father."

"I'm sorry about everything that happened. Lilian was a kind girl. She was never meant for the life of a Black Fist."

Jie shook her head. "She hid so much from us. Her last plan was worthy of the Architect, the manipulation worthy of the Beauty, and the execution worthy of the Surgeon. It was only her affection for me that kept her from escaping after her successful assassination."

"Then you did the right thing in killing her. A renegade to the clan would be a dangerous asset for an ambitious lord."

The truth of his words didn't make it hurt less. Jie sucked on her lower lip.

"Speaking of which," he said, "have you made any headway into finding her employer?"

Jie's gaze raked over all the evidence. "I've tracked the men's families and pored through the records. My working theory is that it was one of the lords of the North."

"I've brought someone for you to train," Master Yan said, his face betraying no emotion.

"Another?" Jie glared at him for the first time in her life. Who was it this time? Little Fei? Little Mai? They'd all be reaching the age when they'd enter the Floating World as embedded Black Lotus sisters. "Father, we need to rethink our approach to the Floating World. How many girls are another Lilian, waiting to happen?"

"I will allow you to speak to the Elders." He gave her the same inscrutable look as always. "For now, though, I brought you an initiate with a preternatural ability to draw connections."

She cocked her head.

He stepped aside, revealing a quivering boy of no older than ten years. "This is Zheng Tian."

The boy's lips trembled, and he ducked behind Master Yan.

"He's a little shy." Master Yan gave a rare smile, then nudged the boy forward and pointed at the open ledgers. "Little Tian, what do you make of that?"

The boy's eyes darted to Jie before roving over the figures. He stammered as he said, in a tremulous voice, "These companies paid for the party for Lord Peng, who is from the South. They all operate in the North."

"How can you tell they operate in the North?" Master Yan asked.

"Jinjing Lumber Company—Jinjing is a county in the North. Luo Trading—it imports from the foreigners in the North."

Jie gawked. In just three seconds, the boy had deduced what had taken her days to research. He might not have all the answers now, but with more training, maybe he would.

And she could find out who had turned Lilian.

***

Find out who was behind the assassination in **White Sheep of the Family**.

Turn to the next page for a bonus short story, and an excerpt from **White Sheep of the Family**.

MISDIRECTION:

A Scions of the Black Lotus Short Story

A Seedling's first months in the Floating World were supposed to be tortuous, as their Gardener broke their will. Until now eight-year-old Yuna had found it quite relaxing.

Really, being forced to scrub the floors of the common room on her hands and knees was nothing compared to calisthenics back at the Black Lotus Temple, and being punished with a flogger felt like a tickle after undergoing the clan's torture-resistance training.

Now, though, cell leader Jie had given her the most onerous task.

With the wood planks of the safehouse hallway cool beneath her feet, she sidestepped the incoming knife stab. She slashed at Zheng Tian's palmar tendons. Had they been using live blades, the banished lordling would've never held a weapon again. Instead, the resin on her practice blade left a black mark.

Dunderhead that he was, instead of switching his knife to his other hand like he was supposed to, he pressed his offense.

His attack slipped past her guard. She braced for the impact on her chest.

It didn't come. He'd pulled up.

The dunderhead! If he was going to break the rules, he should at least respect her enough to finish the blow. With a flick of her wrist, she jabbed at his ribs with the *No-Shadow Cut.*

It hit!

Maybe having to spar with Tian wasn't so bad. The technique she'd been so close to landing had actually hit! She was now the youngest to ever accomplish it. She looked sidelong at Jie, who before this moment had been the youngest to accomplish the difficult move.

"Point, Yuna." The half-elf was beaming. It might have been the first time she'd smiled since Lilian's death, which made Yuna happier than scoring the point.

"Wow, I didn't see that coming." Tian stepped back and rubbed the spot. He moved his hand, revealing the black mark on his white padded armor.

Yuna's shoulders slumped. She'd been close, but he had so much baby fat, she'd misjudged the target.

"But what about my point?" Tian asked.

Jie shook her head. "You didn't land the blow."

"I didn't want to hurt her. Father says—"

Jie held up a hand. "Forget what your father says. Great Lords follow Great Rules. You are now an initiate of the Black Lotus Clan. Now, what was your first mistake?"

Yuna gritted her teeth. Tian would get the next answer wrong.

"Not finishing the attack?"

"No!" Jie threw up her hands.

He scratched his chin. Apparently, no answer was forthcoming.

Jie rolled her eyes. "You treated her like a girl."

"She *is* a girl," he said with genuine confusion.

"A girl who would've crippled you for life," Yuna muttered under her breath. "And it would've been a short life."

Jie shook her head. "Zheng Tian, we must consider everyone a potential threat, even a child."

Looking at Yuna, Tian bobbed his head. "I understand."

Did he? Yuna frowned at him, tempted to try a *No-Shadow Cut* again.

"Good," Jie said. "Now Yuna, take Tian to the drop-off."

"Drop-off?" Tian asked, excitement in his voice.

"What?" Yuna gawked. Though was a minor assignment, meant more for training, having this incompetent boy along would blow even this simple mission.

"You are responsible for him. He has to pick the locks and make the drop-off."

Yuna's heart sank, but complaining would do no good. As numb as Jie was these days, it would be better not to give her more pressure. Scowling at Tian, she pulled off her own padded armor. Beneath it was her stealth suit, since she'd snuck out of the Peony Garden tonight.

Tian, on the other hand, wore plain laborer's clothes under his armor.

A boy so poorly dressed would have no business where they were going, and he didn't know anything about either fitting in or melting into shadows.

In the corner of her eye, Jie was peering back.

Oh, the half-elf was testing *her*. See if she could get Tian into the drop-off point without being spotted.

Well, a plan was already forming.

Jie scribbled out a message on a sheet of paper that came out of nowhere. She folded it up and set in

Yuna's palm. "You have until a count of… a thousand."

Given Yuna's best time was a third of that, this was unusually generous. No doubt their courageous cell leader knew Tian would slow Yuna down.

"What happens if we don't finish in time?" Tian asked, voice tremulous.

Jie would usually grin, now her lips just pressed tight. "For every second late, you'll have to squat for a minute in a horse stance, arms outstretched, balancing a teacup on your head and knees, with a candle under your butt."

A common punishment back at the temple, it also served the dual purpose of training muscles. Yuna hadn't been subjected to it in years. But now that she was responsible for Tian, her joints ached in anticipation.

Tian gulped. "What is the mission?"

"The first part is getting past the rear door." Yuna led him in a sprint through the hall until they came to a long stretch that ended with a mural of a dragon. Already, she'd counted to fifteen. "Now, notice how I test the pressure of the floorboards."

Eyes wide, he watched as she pressed her foot in one spot. It started to let out a little chirp, so she eased up. She slid her foot over to the safe spot and stepped.

"Oh!" he said. "My father has nightingale floors in his castle."

"Of course he does, and I'm sure you just chirp-chirped across them with those heavy feet of yours." Knowing the thirty-seven safe spots, she zig-zagged over the joists and joints. Count of seventy-two, about the same as usual for her.

Behind her, Tian's footfalls made it sound like he was backing up and going for a running jump. That would save time, but there was no way he could cover the entire hall. When she reached the end of the hall, she turned and looked back. "Now— "

Tian was already halfway down the path. It looked like he was following in her footsteps, which should be nearly impossible considering how many there were and how fast she'd taken them. While his larger size led to audible steps, the floorboards didn't chirp.

"You're not supposed to...you need to test for chirps!" she hissed.

Not heeding her words, he arrived at her side, panting.

A hundred and twelve. They were actually on pace for her usual time. "How did you do that?"

"Do what?"

"Memorize my steps?"

He shrugged. "I don't know. I just...did?"

Maybe Tian was smarter than he looked. She turned around to look at the wall.

"What are you looking for?" Tian peered at the painting. "It's just a picture."

"Is it?" Grinning, Yuna brought her finger to one of the dragon scales. "See the shading here? It conceals a lock. You'll see this in some wealthy merchants' homes."

His lips rounded. "Jie said I have to pick it."

Yuna withdrew two of her tools from her hair and gave them to him. This would easily eat up a count of fifty or so.

He grabbed them like a starving man reaching for a steamed bun that had fallen on the ground. "What do I do?"

At least he was enthusiastic. "Use that one to put a little torsion on the cylinder. Good. Now, use the pick to place pressure on the tumblers."

Tian did as he was told, and even with his pudgy fingers, he was doing admirably for his first time.

"You have to feel it," she said, counting to two hundred and three. "The little pressure. It imitates the shape of the key."

Snick. The lock yielded.

"I think I did it?"

That was fast; certainly quicker than the first time she'd unlocked this door. "Not bad, but that was the easiest lock to pick. Now—"

He pushed on the door and it opened. Smoothly at first, but then it creaked.

"That noise adds a count of five." She shook her head. "Always remember, push a little to test the hinges. If they squeak, you need to oil them. It's our habit to only open them as wide as we must to slip out." Which for him was probably twice as wide as for her.

"Why is this called a drop-off?" he asked.

"You'll see." With a sigh, she quickly wrapped a sash over his eyes, then her own.

"What are you doing?" he said.

"We must navigate the next route using all senses except sight."

"That's not possible!"

Yuna snorted. "At the temple, we spend a year blindfolded."

"I didn't!"

"Calm down." It was hard to believe Tian was older than her. "Feel with your feet and hands. Listen. Smell."

"Okay, I think I can do that."

"Here's a trick." One which would help steepen his learning curve. Still, they were packing years of training into a few minutes. "Hum, and sense how the sound changes as we walk through the hall."

"All right."

"You go first." She reached back and pulled Tian forward.

Humming, Yuna prodded him. They'd already reached a count of three hundred and sixteen.

His feet shuffled forward.

Three paces in, she said, "Do you hear how the pitch changes to our right?"

"Yes," he said, enthusiasm rising in his voice.

"Jie has set up a folding screen there. Press your back to the left and sidle by."

From the shift in her hum, she could tell he was doing as she said. She followed along. Up ahead, there was a chest…

"There's something on the floor," Tian said, voice satisfied. He started to step over it.

Something shifted in her hum. She pushed back against the wall. A soft thump sent Tian tripping over the chest on the floor between them. He reeled back.

She just avoided him, and shot a hand out to catch his wrist. His weight jarred her arm, but she kept him from falling.

"What was that?" he demanded.

"A swinging canvas bag, filled with mung beans," Jie's voice said from up ahead. "And a ten-second penalty."

Yuna grit her teeth. With the penalty, they were now nearing a count of five hundred. "Just a few more steps. I'll take the lead."

"I'm not going to be hit by something from behind, am I?"

Yuna laughed. "You know me too well already. But no."

They made it to the second secret door, and she pulled off the blindfold. Five hundred and forty-one.

Tian was already scanning the wall. He pointed to the hidden keyhole. "That's the lock, isn't it?"

"Yes," Yuna said. "But—"

He inserted the picks.

Snick!

He jerked his hand back. "Ow!"

"—always check for traps." Sighing, she shook her head. She couldn't fault his enthusiasm.

"Another ten-second penalty," Jie's voice echoed from somewhere.

"You should've told me earlier!" Tian whipped his hand back and forth.

"I tried!" Yuna leaned in and inspected the drop of blood on Tian's finger. "It's a spring-loaded dart. Sometimes they are poisoned."

Tian pouted. "Does that mean the half-elf wants you to fail in the drop-off?"

"She can hear you, you know." Yuna laughed.

He covered his mouth.

"No, though. This is a non-critical mission, just for training." She nodded toward the door.

This time he tested the hinges, then opened it just wide enough for him to squeeze through. At least he learned quickly. Six hundred.

She walked out and joined him at the top of a flight of stairs, which was lit by light bauble lamps. This would be where they'd lose most of her time. "Now, stairs are like floors. They can creak. You have to test each one. Every creak loses us ten seconds. Go on."

With a nod, he set one foot on the first stair and shifted his weight onto it. When it didn't squeak, he stepped onto it with both feet and looked back at her.

"Good," she said." Keep going."

She waited at the top as he continued, easing up whenever a tread started to creak. Eventually, he made it down the thirteen steps to the door at the bottom, only making the stairs squeak once.

Leaping up, she shot her arms and legs out so that the pressure of her hands and feet on the wall kept her above the steps. She spider-climbed down in a count of ten, bring their total to six hundred and sixty-eight.

"Hey! Isn't that cheating?"

She snorted. "Haven't you figured it out yet? There's no such thing as cheating. What matters are the results."

"But Father says..."

"Is your father a Black Fist who stabs people in the back?"

Tian shook his head.

Yuna jabbed him in the ribs with a finger. "You now are. So forget his lessons in honor."

Rubbing his chest, Tian gave her a wounded look.

Her stomach twisted. The poor boy had been banished and was missing his parents. Well, she couldn't afford to show softness, lest he never grow up. She hardened her expression. "In any case, you're free to try what I just did the next time."

Head hanging, he turned away and inspected the door. He found the lock, checked for traps, and then picked it. Each time, he was getting faster and more efficient. He opened the door wide enough for him, letting in a waft of heady scents. Seven hundred and two.

"What is this place?" he asked.

"What do you think?"

He sniffed the air. "It smells like my grandma."

She chuckled. "Go on."

He slipped through, and she followed, closing the door behind her. Five paces away, on the opposite wall, strings of beads dangled from an open doorway. It let in enough light from the space beyond to shine on crates of herbs.

"A pharmacy?" he whispered.

Yuna nodded.

"Are we dropping off a prescription?"

"One that will shut you up," she hissed.

He bowed his head, contrite, and followed her as she crept over to the doorway. She looked between the hanging beads.

A male customer stood close by, between two rows of sealed jars and pill boxes. Past him, at the front of the pharmacy, the herbalist stood behind a counter, weighing out herbs on a hanging scale. A second customer stood across from him, arms folded over his chest. Seven hundred and twenty-nine.

"What now?" Tian whispered.

"You need to sneak by everyone and leave the message on the counter."

"Then what happens?"

She pressed the missive into his palm. "A clan courier will pick it up."

"Won't the herbalist unwrap the message?"

"He's a Cousin."

"What's that?"

All these questions were wasting time. "He was once an initiate, like you, but failed. Now, thanks to the *Tiger's Eye*, he has no memories of ever being with us. Still, he knows to leave the paper there."

Tian swallowed hard and nodded.

"All right," she said, resigned to not making the time. "I will sneak past everyone and out the front door, and then create a diversion. When no one is looking, you drop the message off."

Up front, the herbalist was finishing with the customer.

"I think..." Tian started.

"Just do as I say." Dropping to her stomach, Yuna shimmied out under the beads. She stood and slipped around a row of drying herbs dangling from the ceiling. With the shelves blocking lines of sight, she stayed low and darted toward the front. She could slip out when the customer left, using the jangle of bells to cover her escape. Count of nine hundred seventy-two.

She turned and beckoned for Tian to—

He wasn't there. She bobbed up to peek over the shelf.

Tian walked past the first customer, who paid him no mind, then right up to the counter. No, no, no, what was he thinking? They'd lose the challenge, which would mean an hour of horse stances over candles.

The herbalist looked up from his work. "Welcome. How may I help you?"

Tian set the message on the table. "I am dropping off an herbal formula for my master."

The herbalist reached for it.

Tian shook his head and held out a hand. "You're busy. No hurry. He wants to watch you mix it. He will be here shortly. I just got here early. So I could choose some medicinal wines." He pointed his thumb at the shelves of jars near the rear.

The herbalist nodded and went back to his work.

Tian went toward the rear of the shop, then crawled under the bead curtain.

Fuming, Yuna joined him. "If you make a sound, I'm going to beat you myself."

He started to speak, but then sealed his lips tight.

She grabbed his ear and pulled him through the room and back up the steps. At the top, she poked him in the ribs. "Count of one thousand and three! And you were noticed, which means extra punishment. What were you thinking?"

"But...we just had to drop off the message, right?"

"Yes, but..."

"You said rules didn't matter, just results. The courier will still get his message, and for all anyone knows, a boy just dropped off a prescription."

Yuna started to say something, then shut her mouth. He wasn't wrong.

"And I'll deduct ten seconds for creativity," Jie said.

A grin came to Yuna's lips, unbidden. Tian might be annoying, but he wasn't totally clueless. Maybe he wouldn't be so bad to have around after all.

WHITE SHEEP OF THE FAMILY: EXCERPT

Before yesterday, ten-year-old Zheng Tian had always believed Black Fists to be a fairy tale: mythical villains meant to scare children into good behavior.

Now bruised and panting, he backed up and lowered his sword. He couldn't say he'd never been bested by a girl two years younger and head shorter—only twenty-seven days had passed since the last instance— but this was the first time an opponent had worn a blindfold *and* a dress, and made such short work of him.

"You won." He hung his head and saluted with a fist in an open palm.

Yuna, his skinny vanquisher, removed the blindfold and returned the gesture. "Thank you for letting me."

That typical polite response. He'd heard it many times over the years, and it stung more than ever now.

"I'll need to work out the other shoulder to keep the muscles balanced." Jie, the cruel half-elf girl judging the match, rolled her left shoulder. She'd raised that arm each time the eight-year-old scored a point, seventeen times in all.

Tian frowned. His arms ached, too, albeit from the weight of the practice sword.

"Yuna, you may go." Jie saluted. She didn't look much older than either Yuna or him, yet somehow she was in charge of his new world. "Your list for next time is, red, sword, wheel, dagger, green, stab, cloudy, spicy, crossbow, opera, bludgeon, slippery, sun, finger, six, two, zero, nine."

Closing her eyes, the girl mouthed the words. Then, she bobbed her head in the cutest way, less like the swordswoman who'd thrashed him, more like Princess Kaiya.

Tian's stomach twisted. Four days. It'd been four days since he'd last since the love of his life, the girl he'd promised to marry. The girl he'd never see again. Four days since his banishment from the capital.

Once Yuna left the small, sunlit room, Jie turned back to him. There was nothing cute about her, except maybe those pointed ears. Her gaze bore into him. "Zheng Tian, why did you lose?"

Why, indeed? He shouldn't have, given his opponent's stance and shorter reach. Maybe if there'd been more space. He stretched his arms out to the side, demonstrating the narrowness of the wood-floored chamber. "There's no room."

"If you get attacked in an alley, are you going to ask your assailant to take it out into the street?"

He started to respond, but closed his mouth. There was more than just the amount of space. He pointed to the window. "The sun was in my eyes."

It also cast Jie's hair in a unique shade of dark brown, unlike any other in a realm of black-haired people. "She was blindfolded."

The humiliation still stung, but there was more. His shoes' smooth soles had slipped more than once. "The floor was too slick."

The evil half-elf rolled her eyes. "You fought on the same floor."

"She was barefooted!"

"Nobody said you had to wear shoes."

All the disadvantages, this one self-imposed. Still, despite him preempting all Yuna's possible lines of attack and defense, she always landed a quick, decisive blow. His sword, in contrast, might've been as sluggish as a water buffalo. "Yuna was holding her sword in stance six. But then, she used pattern two."

"And?"

"You're not supposed to mix the two. Every sword master says so."

"You're overanalyzing." Jie threw her hands up—the right higher than the left, proving her muscles were already balanced. "Swordplay isn't forensic accounting."

Whatever forensic meant, and what it had to do with counting, had to be better than getting beaten by an eight-year-old, blindfolded girl. He shook his head. "Her moves didn't match her stance. It's not fair."

"Exactly!" The evil half-elf's lip quirked. "Had we been using real blades, you'd be dead a twenty times over."

"Seventeen. Fifteen, because two weren't fatal blows."

Jie blew out a frustrated breath.

Tian's shoulders slumped. There was no denying the truth. "Yuna's better with a sword."

"I was waiting for that answer." Jie's smile looked less kindly, and more like a the God of the Underworld bargaining for souls.

This had all been a lesson. These new teachers had to break him down before building him back—

"But no. You're the son of a hereditary lord. You've learned from great sword masters, and your technique is superior for your age. You have a longer reach and a size advantage. You might even be better than me." She sucked on her lower lip. "Well, maybe not..."

Tian looked up. "The Founder wrote in the Art of War that knowing your enemy—"

"—will win you half your battles. Yes, yes." Jie held up a hand. "I'm glad you can recite the Founder. What did he say about choosing your battlefield?"

His mouth formed a circle of its own accord. It all made sense. "The narrow space limited what I could do, and neutralized my reach advantage. The slick floors slowed my reaction. Yuna kept the sunlight in my face to make up for the blindfold—"

Jie shook her head. "We will teach you to fight in the dark, using all your senses. But what you should get out of this is, forget everything you learned about duels. We don't fight fair. Do you remember how heavy your sword felt?"

"Yes."

"Yuna gave you the one with a lead core."

And when she did, she'd hefted it as if it were light. He made several slow nods. Really, he'd only lost his duels to Princess Kaiya because she didn't fight fair, either, and he let her get away with it. Out of love.

"But most importantly, don't analyze in the heat of the moment. Turn your brain off, and let your reflexes take over."

"I will try."

When Jie smiled instead of smirked, it was like sunlight peeking out through the clouds on a rainy day. "There's hope for you yet."

***

White Sheep of the Family, available now.

Join my mailing list (http://eepurl.com/c5rssT) and get a FREE copy of **Prelude to Insurrection**, a story about Tian and Jie ten years after **Thorn of the Night Blossoms**.

APPENDICES

Celestial Bodies

White Moon: Known as Renyue in Cathay, and represents the God of the Seas. Its orbital period is thirty days.

Iridescent Moon: Known in Cathay as Caiyue, it is the manifestation of the God of Magic. It appeared at the end of the war between elves and orcs. It never moves from its spot in the sky. Its orbital period is one day, and can be used to keep time.

Blue Moon: Known in Cathay as Guanyin's Eye, it is the manifestation of the Goddess of Fertility. Its phases go from wide open to winking.

Tivar's Star: A red star, a manifestation of the God of Conquest. During the Year of the Second Sun, it approached the world, causing the Blue Moon to go dim.

Hunter Kor: A constellation, always in pursuit of the White Stag

Lycea the Betrayer: A star, avatar of the Goddess of Betrayals

White Stag: A constellation, always hiding from Hunter Kor

Fortuna: A constellation of the Goddess of Luck

Time

As measured by the phases of the Iridescent Moon:
Full = Midnight
1st Waning Gibbons = 1:00 AM
2nd Waning Gibbons =2:00 AM
Mid-Waning Gibbons = 3:00 AM
4th Waning Gibbons = 4:00 AM
5th Waning Gibbons = 5:00 AM
Waning Half = 6:00 AM
1st Waning Crescent = 7:00 AM
2nd Waning Crescent = 8:00 AM
Mid-Waning Crescent = 9:00 AM
4th Waning Crescent = 10:00 AM
5th Waning Crescent = 11: 00 AM
New = Noon
1st Waxing Crescent = 1:00 PM
2nd Waxing Crescent = 2:00 PM
Mid-Waxing Crescent = 3:00 PM
4th Waxing Crescent = 4:00 PM
5th Waxing Crescent = 5:00 PM
Waxing Half = 6:00 PM
1st Waxing Gibbons = 7:00 PM
2nd Waxing Gibbons =8:00 PM
Mid-Waxing Gibbons = 9:00 PM
4th Waxing Gibbons = 10:00 PM
5th Waxing Gibbons = 11:00 PM

Human Ethnicities

Aksumi: Dark-skinned with dark eyes and coarse hair. On Earth, they would be considered North Africans. They can use Sorcery.

Ayuri: Bronze-toned skin with dark hair and eyes. On Earth, they would be considered South Asians. They can use Martial Magic.

Arkothi: Olive-skinned with blond to dark hair and light-colored eyes. On Earth, they would be considered Eastern Mediteraneans. They can use Rune Magic.

Bovyan: The descendants of the Sun God's begotten son, they are cursed to be all male and live only to thirty-three years of age. They are much taller and larger than the average human. Their other physical characteristics are determined by their mother's race. They have no magical ability.

Cathayi (Hua): Honey-toned skin with dark hair and eyes. High-set cheekbones and almond-shaped eyes. On Earth, they would be considered East Asians. They can use Artistic Magic.

Eldaeri: Olive-skinned with brown hair. With features and small frames, they are shorter in stature than the average human. In a previous age, they fled the orc domination of the continent and mingled with elves. They have no magical ability.

Estomari: Olive-skinned with varying eye and hair color. They are famous for their fine arts. On Earth, they would be considered Western Mediterraneans. They can use Divining Magic.

Kanin: Ruddy-skinned with dark hair. On Earth, they would be considered Native Americans. They can use Shamanic Magic.

Levanthi: Dark-bronze skin and dark hair. On Earth, they would be considered Persians. They can use Divine Magic.

Nothori: fair-skinned and fair-haired. On Earth, they would be considered Northern Europeans. They can use Empathic Magic.

Acknowledgements

First, I would like to thank my wife and family for the patience they have afforded me as I pursued my childhood dream of fiction writing.

A shout-out goes to my old Dungeons and Dragons crew: Jon, Chris, Chris, Paul, Conrad, and Julian, for helping to shape the first iteration of Tivara twenty-five years ago. Huge thanks to Brent, who contributed so much backstory to the new literary version.

A huge thanks to my sister Laura for her spectacular job with the maps.

And finally, an even huger thanks to the readers of The Dragon Songs Saga who contacted me, wanting to know more about Jie. You are the reason this book happened.

ABOUT THE AUTHOR

JC Kang's unhealthy obsession with Fantasy and Sci-Fi began at an early age when his brother introduced him to The Chronicles of Narnia, Star Trek, and Star Wars. As an adult, he combines his geek roots with his professional experiences as a Chinese Medicine doctor, martial arts instructor, and technical writer to pen epic fantasy stories.

Made in the USA
Columbia, SC
20 November 2020